The Swingers III & IV

Public Affairs
Coming through the Rye

NICK CLARKE

BLUE MOON BOOKS
NEW YORK

The Swingers III & IV
Copyright © 1993, 2005 by Potiphar Productions

Published by
Blue Moon Books
An Imprint of Avalon Publishing Group Incorporated
245 West 17th Street, 11th floor
New York, NY 10011-5300

First Blue Moon Books Edition 2005

First Published in 1993 by Simon & Schuster Ltd

ISBN 1-56201-470-6

9 8 7 6 5 4 3 2 1

Printed in Canada
Distributed by Publishers Group West

PUBLIC AFFAIRS

This is for Heather Shackleton

Shift and shirt are off together
　　Naked is the sweet embrace;
Not one part's concealed by either,
　　All's as naked as your face.

Give me then, ten thousand kisses,
　　Give me all your blooming charms;
Give me heavenly, melting blisses,
　　Lying naked in my arms!

Sir Lionel Trapes (1826–1908)

❀ CHAPTER ONE ❀

That Was A Week, That Was

'What's the difference between an egg and a blow job?' asked Brian Lipman as the photographer plonked his ample frame into the chair opposite Ivor Belling's desk and handed his client a sheaf of colour prints.

'I don't know, Brian, enlighten me,' grinned Ivor Belling as he leafed through the set of photographs.

'You can beat an egg,' came the quick reply and the two men guffawed whilst Suzie, Ivor's new secretary, came into the office and set down two mugs of tea and a plate of biscuits on a table just in front of Brian Lipman, who smacked his lips and said: 'My, my, Cadbury's chocolate fingers and it's not even Friday afternoon! We're really pushing the boat out today, business must be picking up. Who knows, I might even live long enough to see Cable Publicity settle my account in thirty days.'

'Oh dear, didn't Mr Green in accounts give you a cheque this morning?' said Suzie sadly, looking reproachfully at Ivor. 'Well, at least have another biscuit, Brian.'

'Hey, don't make the bugger too comfortable or he'll call round every afternoon,' Ivor protested which caused the pretty, raven-haired girl to smile and say: 'Don't worry, it's just a little bribe to get him to take my passport photographs free of charge.'

Ivor looked up with a slightly worried expression on his face. 'Passport photographs, Suzie? Christ, I hope you're

1

not planning to take a holiday in the near future; you know how busy we'll be for the next couple of months.'

'Listen, the girl's entitled to a holiday,' Brian Lipman protested volubly. 'Ivor, this is 1966 and the times when you could grind the workers' faces into the ground are long, long gone. Suzie darling, if this hard-hearted capitalist doesn't give you the time off to which you're entitled, go on strike.'

'Thank you, comrade, well said,' said Ivor heavily. 'I'm so pleased to hear you speak up. Do you know, I never knew till now just how concerned you are about the welfare of our employees. Come to think of it, I didn't even know it was any of your business as you only work for us in a freelance capacity. But if our working practices offend you, please feel free to withdraw your services. I'm sure we'll find another photographer who'll work at your extortionate rates.'

'Extortionate rates?' echoed the photographer, feigning an expression of affronted surprise. 'I could get double the fees from J. Walter Thompson for the same stuff I do for you – and I'd probably get paid a bloody sight quicker too!'

Suzie looked up in concern but her brow cleared when she saw the two men grinning at each other and she realised that the argument was simply friendly banter and her mention of an intended vacation had not in any way affected the long-standing friendship of her boss, Ivor Belling, the deputy managing director of Cable Publicity, a small but thriving public relations agency and Brian Lipman, a commercial photographer whose basement studio in Holborn was just five minutes walk away from Cable's offices and where Ivor and Brian enjoyed occasional steamy sex sessions with several obliging models eager to further their careers.

Yet Suzie was still concerned and she looked at her employer anxiously and said: 'I've already booked two weeks in August for my summer holiday, Ivor, but I do want to leave at lunchtime on Friday afternoon because I'm going to France for the weekend. Warren, my boy friend, is driving over and we want to catch the four o'clock ferry from Dover. He has to stay in Paris for a few days but I'll get a train back on Sunday afternoon so I'll be in at the usual time on Monday.'

'You're leaving it a bit late to get a new passport, Suzie,' commented Lipman. 'I'm working late tonight. Come down to the studio after work and I'll take the photograph for you so you can have the prints tomorrow.'

'Thanks, Brian, I'm really grateful,' she said with relief. 'It's my own silly fault that I'm in such a panic. I only noticed yesterday that my passport's out of date. Now I can go to the Passport Office in my lunch hour tomorrow and go down on my bended knees and ask them to speed through my new one.'

'Well, you don't have to go down on your bended knees in front of me, though I won't object if you want to,' chuckled the ever randy Brian Lipman and Suzie smiled saucily back at him. 'I don't think Warren would appreciate it if I did,' she said with a twinkle in her eye. 'Of course, if you want to change his mind, you're welcome to try but I've told you before, he's six foot two, built like the proverbial brick outhouse and I couldn't answer for the consequences if he really lost his temper with another man.'

'Another time, perhaps, when Warren's out of town – preferably when he's rowing round Cape Horn in a storm,' said the photographer hastily.

Ivor blew out his cheeks and leaned back in his chair. 'There's no problem as far as I'm concerned, Suzie, if you want to leave early on Friday, except that you must thoroughly check all the arrangements for the Four Seasons dog food press conference up in Scotland before you leave. Remember, Brian and I are booked on the Sunday night sleeper to Glasgow.

'We can't afford any slip-ups as we dreamed up the

3

whole campaign, and the client's advertising agency would love to see us with egg on our faces so that they could pitch for the public relations business themselves as they've just set up their own PR agency.'

'Don't worry, Trish hasn't much to do whilst Martin is in Birmingham most of this week and she said that she'll give me a hand when we do a final ring-round tomorrow. You don't mind if she comes to the studio with me this evening, do you, Brian? We're having a quick bite at Yummies and then we're going on to the pictures afterwards.'

'No, of course not, it'll only take two minutes to take the photographs. Be at the studio at about six o'clock and you can pick up the prints at half past eleven tomorrow morning,' said Brian Lipman with a farewell wave of the hand as Suzie dashed to the door to answer her telephone in the outlying office.

'She's a nice kid,' he added to Ivor who wagged a finger at him. 'Hands off, Brian, she's a good secretary and I want her to stay. So just point your Hassalblad at her this evening.'

'Relax, my friend, I don't think I could do more than raise my hand even if Sophia Loren walked in naked tonight and asked me if I would be kind enough to fuck her.'

Ivor scratched his head, 'I thought you were having dinner with your parents last night,' he said with a puzzled expression. 'Did your mother's *gefilte* fish keep you up all night?'

The photographer laughed and gulped down a great draught of tea from his mug. 'You could say so, in an indirect kind of way. You see I went to my parents to meet a second cousin from New York, a girl called Vivienne Rosen who I'd never heard of before, who had written to my mother saying she was coming to London. Naturally my mother asked her to come for dinner and I was roped in to meet the lady.

'Truthfully, I wasn't looking forward to spending an

evening sitting around making polite conversation about all our American relatives, but then I'm probably going to America next year and it's much cheaper to stay with a cousin than in a hotel! Anyhow, she was there when I arrived and what a pleasant surprise! Vivienne was a real corker, about twenty-five, very pretty with long dark hair to her shoulders, and she was wearing a little red mini-skirt with black seamed stockings which rippled up her long legs when she walked towards me.

'"Hi Brian, nice to meet you. I've heard an awful lot about you from Auntie Bessie," she said pleasantly as we shook hands. "You know, I work in public relations and I want to tell you that your ma would make a great press agent."

'"Don't I know it," I said, looking appreciatively at Vivienne's pointy breasts. "According to her, David Bailey, Karsh of Ottawa and Mark Gerson ring me up when they need expert advice."

'Anyhow, to cut a long story short, my long-lost second cousin and I got on like a house on fire – so much so that by the time my mother brought in her famous *lockshen* pudding, Vivienne had slipped off her shoe and under the cover of the tablecloth was moving her silk-clad foot up and down my leg. I stole her the odd steamy glance when my parents weren't looking but I can tell you that my prick was threatening to burst out of my trousers! Far from bothering her, when coffee was served Vivienne deliberately looked down at my crotch when she leaned over me to take the sugar bowl and an amused look came over her face and her moist, pink tongue came out to lick her lips.

'Vivienne had taken a taxi to Golders Green but of course when I could decently say it was time to go, I insisted on driving her back to her hotel just off Baker Street. "Must you go so soon?" said my father but Vivienne was as keen as me to leave and just as I started the car she said: "Do you live nearby, Brian? I'd love to see your apartment. Would you mind if I had a look round it before we go back to the hotel?"

' "You took the words out of my mouth," I said happily and with Vivienne's head snuggled down on my shoulder, I drove out to my new pad in Elstree. Once safely inside we took off our jackets and I offered her a drink whilst I put on my new Duke Ellington LP. "Not just now thank you, Brian, but can I take a rain check for later?" she smiled and as she moved closer I caught a whiff of her delicious perfume. She clutched my upper arm with both hands and I turned her face up towards mine and we kissed.

'Well, I honestly only intended a gentle kiss at first but from the moment our lips touched it was obvious that we were going to pass the *hors d'oeuvres* and move straight away to the main course. Her mouth opened and almost sucked in my willing tongue from its roots! Her soft body pressed against me and she started to rub her pubes against my rock hard boner.

'We fell backwards on to the couch and I feverishly unbuttoned her sparkling white cotton blouse which she slipped off and Vivienne unhooked her bra herself, sliding the straps off her shoulders and as our lips mashed together I caressed her naked breasts in my hand, squeezing, rubbing and flicking the red stalky nipples with my fingers.

'Meanwhile, Vivienne's hand snaked downwards and drew down the zip of my trousers. She reached inside and pulled out my rock-hard stiffie. "My, you're well endowed," she said softly as she weighed my shaft up in her palm and clasped both her hands round my throbbing tool and I groaned as she leaned forward and let the tip of her tongue wash all over my knob. She moved from my side and unzipped her skirt, letting it fall to her ankles. She stepped out of it and I nearly came there and then as I ran my eyes over her firm, tanned body which was now naked except for a brief pink pantie-girdle with suspenders which Vivienne detached as she sat down on the floor and took off her stockings. Then she stood up, wriggled out of her girdle and stood totally nude for a moment before falling to her knees in front of me and taking hold of my bursting cock, drew in my bell-end between her lips, licking and lapping as she crammed inch after inch of my prick further back into her throat. My God, Ivor, my American cousin certainly knew how to such a cock!

'I groaned with pleasure when her magic tongue circled my knob and her teeth scraped the tender flesh as she drew me in between those luscious lips, stroking her tongue up and down the underside of my cock, making it ache with excitement whilst she cupped my tightening balls in her hands, sucking harder and harder until I gasped out: "A-a-a-h! That's fantastic, darling! It feels so good! Oh Christ, I'm coming! I'm coming!"

'I tried to pull my prick away because I thought she might want me to come outside her mouth but no, she slid her hands under my bum and pulled me backwards and forwards until with a final throb I shot my load into her mouth. She gulped down my spunk and licked all round my knob to gather up the last drains before she looked up and said: "M'mmm, that was delicious, Brian, even tastier than your ma's *lockshen* pudding. But now I want you to fuck me."'

Ivor burst out laughing and said: 'Dear me! Immediately after such a great blow job? I suppose you had to copy those Sunday newspaper reporters who write that just when the girl offers herself they make their excuses and leave!'

Brian Lipman joined in the laughter but shook his head. 'No fear, I wasn't going to miss out just because I'm not seventeen years old any more, when I could come three times without losing my hard-on. I pulled Vivienne down onto the couch and we kissed and cuddled until I recovered. Whilst we petted, I diddled her pussy, sliding one, two and finally three fingers inside her cunt. I finger-fucked her as she frigged my stiffening shaft inside her fist, rubbing it up until it stood as hard as iron. It didn't take long before she was lying on her back with her legs apart crying out: "Fuck me, fuck me, I can't wait any longer!"

and I was slipping my knob between her pouting pussy lips inside her hairy snatch. Her love box was well lubricated by now and after just a stroke or two my cock was drenched with her juices.

'I kept up a steady rhythm, varying the length of my strokes and shifting my position from time to time to make sure I was really reaming out her honeypot, and she yelped with glee as I pumped away, pressing herself upwards to make certain that every inch of my thick prick was inside her. She opened her legs wide and then wrapped them round my waist as a great shiver tore through her entire body and she screamed out: "I'm there! I'm there! Shoot your spunk, you big-cocked boy!"

'This helped to finish me off and after a few short, sharp thrusts in and out of her sopping cunt I jetted out my jism in her cunny. I collapsed on top of her but at her request, after a coffee and a large brandy, I lay back and let Vivienne run her tongue down my body, across my chest and around my belly button. My cock began to rise again as she brushed her cheek against the swelling shaft whilst she caressed my heavy, hanging balls with her wet lips.

'She was an athletic girl, Ivor, because even though she must have been as physically tired as me, quick as a flash she slid on top of me, searching for my lips and as we kissed passionately, we moved our thighs together so our pubic muffs rubbed roughly against each other. My prick probed the entrance to her eager little crack and she moaned with delight as my knob forced its way between her cunny lips, massaging her clitty as I arched my body upwards.

'"Oh Brian, keep sliding that lovely cock in and out! What a marvellous lover you are! More! More! Don't stop!" she panted whilst she bounced up and down on my tingling prick and her teeth flashed in a lustful smile. I felt her cunny muscles contract and relax as she rocked up and down on my rock-hard rammer, and I flexed myself to thrust rhythmically into her silky wetness every time she pumped her tight little bum cheeks furiously up and down, digging her fingernails into my flesh as she held on to my body. Each shove was accompanied by a wail of ecstasy as I grabbed her breasts and brought my head up to lick and lap at those rubbery red nipples.

'It was quite a long fuck but we both began the last ride together and I felt her cunt grip my cock even harder as we entered the final furlong. Vivienne shivered and trembled all over, pulling me in as tightly as possible until, with a final push upwards, I spurted a fountain of sticky sperm into her juicy love box. Vivienne gurgled with joy as the frothy white cream flooded into her and I felt her shudder as she drained me of every last drop of jism.

'We rested for an hour or so and then I fucked her once more before taking her back to her hotel. So I didn't get to bed till half past three this morning and I had to be in the studio at eight o'clock to finish those pack shots for this dog food stunt.'

The photographer paused and slumped back in his chair. Ivor looked at him with a twinkle in his eye. 'Sounds like you had quite a night, Brian. Anyhow, your ma won't be too unhappy, even if this girl tells her what happened – after all, she was a nice Jewish girl and you kept it in the family!' He chuckled heartily at his own joke and picked up the sheaf of prints Brian Lipman had brought with him.

'Here, these shots of the poodle eating the Spring formula Four Seasons food aren't half bad. He looks as if he's tucking into it like there's no tomorrow and I must say I like the way you put the display of tins next to the mutt. Thank God the dog liked the product,' Ivor said approvingly.

'Christ you don't think I was going to take a chance with that Four Seasons stuff, do you?' Brian Lipman snorted with disdain. 'There was half a pound of Harrods' best chopped meat in the bowl. Believe me, I fancied cracking open an egg and making up a nice little steak tartare for myself, but I had to give the bloody dog seconds for the colour slides.'

Ivor drew a deep breath as he studied the photographs. 'Why on earth didn't you take the pack shots directly afterwards?' he demanded. 'That way you wouldn't have had to come in so early this morning.'

'I should have done,' admitted Lipman sheepishly. 'But I got friendly with the girl who brought the poodle along from the agency, so I offered her a drink and one thing led to another . . .'

'It'll fall off one of these days if there's any justice left in the world,' said Ivor, shaking his head. 'I don't know where you get the energy from, Brian, honestly I don't.'

'You're just jealous,' said Lipman cheerfully as he heaved himself up from the chair. 'Seriously, Ivor, tell Dave Green in accounts to bring my account up to date. I've got big expenses too, you know, even though I don't have a shpraunzy office and hot and cold running secretaries at my beck and call all day.'

'All right, all right, I'll tell Dave to draw a cheque tomorrow.'

'What's wrong with right now?'

'He's not in the office today. Gone to Hurst Park races as a matter of fact, with Martin,' said Ivor, rolling his eyes upwards in a gesture of resignation.

Lipman looked at Ivor keenly. Martin Reese was the owner and managing director of Cable Publicity who had promoted Ivor to a seat on the board the previous year. 'Okay for some, I suppose,' he said levelly, correctly sensing that Ivor was not altogether happy with Martin's jaunt as the agency had won two new important new accounts and the work load on Ivor and the staff was genuinely heavy. 'Has Dave gone with instructions to break Martin's wrist if he attempts to cash a cheque with the bookies?'

'I hope so,' said Ivor, rising to his feet. 'To be fair, Martin's taken a prospective client who's keen on the gee-gees and Dave's gone along with him because he loves racing, whilst Martin doesn't know one end of a horse from another and has never had a bet in his life.'

'Best way to be,' said Lipman ruefully. 'I lost twenty quid last week because I followed a tip from my barber who said the horse couldn't lose even if the jockey were blindfolded – which he probably was because the bloody horse is still running.'

'I don't know why people are always keen to pass on these absolute certainties,' said Ivor as he accompanied the plump photographer to the door. 'After all, if you spread the word all over and other punters back it, the odds shorten.'

'They do it for the same reason that these nuts go all around the houses trying to convert everyone to some crackpot religion,' said the photographer. 'Listen, if you believe that a certain horse is going to romp home in a race over which you've no control, it's not much different from believing some way-out crackpot idea like only those who practise hitting themselves three times over the head every Thursday are going to heaven. But it must be so much more comforting if you can persuade other people to believe the same crazy notion. It gives you confidence that you can't be such a *shmo* after all.

'So now I've given you the answer, ask me why I listened to my barber about the certainty for the two-thirty at Haydock?'

'Good point – why did you?' asked Ivor.

'I must be at my most susceptible when a girl's fingers are ruffling through my hair,' reflected Brian Lipman and Ivor raised his eyebrows.

'No, I don't go to a ladies' hairdresser,' said Lipman, lightly punching Ivor's arm as he opened the door. 'I go to Shimmy's Unisex Salon in Maddox Street. It's for men and women and there are a nice couple of girls who do the shampooing, but Shimmy cuts all the men's hair.'

Ivor ran a hand over his own long ash blond hair. 'You know, I could do with a haircut myself and Archie, my old barber up in West Hampstead, is retiring. What's this Shimmy like?'

'As a tipster, fucking awful! But he's a very good hairdresser – your old friend Ruff Trayde the pop singer and all his gang go there.'

'Here, he's not one of those,' said Ivor in some alarm. 'I can't bear these camp places.'

'Why, it's not catching is it? But Shimmy's straight as it happens, and very expensive to boot. I paid two guineas for my haircut and shampoo and that's without giving any tips,' said Lipman, pulling out a card from his jacket. 'I'm told Shimmy shafts all the girls who work there and certain favoured clients also get a look-in when they book a half-hour on the sun-bed. Anyhow, here's his business card. Give him a ring and you can find out for yourself. Thanks for the tea and chocolate biscuits, Ivor. I'll see you at King's Cross on Sunday night if not before. Suzie's given me my ticket so we can meet on the train.'

Ivor went back to his desk and strummed his fingers on the diary. He was taking out a new girl friend tonight, a stunning model named Caroline Winchmore whom he had unsuccessfully badgered for a date for the previous three months, ever since he had heard that her romance with a well-known television producer was coming to an end. He needed a haircut and as he was meeting her after a late afternoon fashion show at Claridges, the nearby venue of Shimmy's would be very convenient. He called the number on the card Lipman had given him but at first the receptionist regretfully informed him that Shimmy was fully booked until the beginning of the following week. Then he heard another voice in the background and she said: 'Hold on a minute, sir, I understand that we have just had a cancellation this evening. Would five-thirty be convenient for you?'

It must be fate, thought Ivor, as he firmed up the appointment and settled down to read his senior executive's draft report on one of his major clients, Thomson and Tagholm, purveyors of fine foods since 1769, which had suddenly woken up to the fact that it desperately needed help in propelling itself into the twentieth century. The account had been won by Ivor, with a little extra help from Barbie and the girls at the Hunkiedorie Club [see 'The Swingers 1: The Mini Mob'] but now a difficult new marketing manager had arrived to replace the compliant George Lucas who, whilst Cable Publicity provided enough pussy for him from the Hunkiedorie, would endorse any proposal made by the agency. But the new Thomson and Tagholm contact, Andrew Edwards, was a young high-flyer made of much sterner stuff than George Lucas, who'd been pleased to take early retirement after thirty-two years service, and demanded more action and less words from Ivor and his team of publicists.

Ivor sighed and called Suzie on the internal telephone system. 'Suzie, ask Ian Hughes to come in for a chat about Thomson and Tagholm first thing tomorrow morning, and could you then come in with your notebook and we'll tackle this load of letters in my "in" tray.'

It was a warm September afternoon and Ivor found it difficult to concentrate on the correspondence and was gratefully aware that he could freewheel in it comfortably. He scanned the low cotton top and the ample breasts of his nineteen-year-old secretary as Suzie brushed back a lock of silky black hair from her face and looked up enquiringly at him.

'Is that the lot?' she asked and Ivor nodded. 'Try and get as many out today as you can, but don't bring the letters in later than five o'clock as I'm leaving the office at ten past five sharp,' he said, gazing at her pert, miniskirted bottom as she walked back to her office.

'Make sure you've got enough stamps as it'll be too late to frank the envelopes, and I'd like you to pop them in the pillar box when you leave,' he called after her, and Suzie assured him that all was well. He wriggled uncomfortably in his chair, suddenly realising that he had a huge hard-on. Perhaps Caroline Winchmore will take care of my cock, he muttered to himself, though as it was their first date, he doubted very much if he would get further than a good-night kiss on the front door step of her King's Road, Chelsea apartment. He forced himself to think about the problems of publicising Thomson and Tagholm's jams and marmalades and how their products could best be brought to the attention of both the grocery trade and the housewives.

The early autumn sunshine shone strongly and Ivor threw open the balcony windows to catch any breath of air, and although the thunder of the High Holborn traffic now beat in, Ivor closed his eyes and enjoyed a short nap before being woken by the shrill ringing of his telephone. He grabbed the receiver and a husky female voice asked: 'Ivor? Is that you? Caroline Winchmore here. Ivor, darling, I'm awfully sorry, I'll have to break our date tonight. There's a party this evening at *Vogue* which my agent says I must go to.'

'Oh, hell's bells, I was really looking forward to seeing you, Caroline,' said Ivor fretfully. 'Look, I'd only booked a table at the Terrazza and I can cancel that easily enough. Can't I come with you to this party?'

There was a short pause on the line and then she said: 'Well, darling, I honestly don't think that it'll be quite your scene, and there'll be oodles of shop talk. I really think it best I take a rain check, if you don't mind.'

Ivor scowled and grit his teeth as he just about managed to keep his rising irritation out of his voice. 'Fair enough, I'll give you a ring when I get back from Scotland on Wednesday afternoon.' It was all he could do to say good-bye civilly before he slammed the phone back on its rack. It was obvious that this party – if indeed it did genuinely exist – was just a bloody excuse and Caroline had probably been propositioned by someone she found more attractive or, very probably, more useful to her, for the majority of models he knew were predatory, ruthless creatures when it came to furthering their careers.

In a black mood he glanced at his watch – should he now cancel his appointment at Shimmy's? Well, what the heck, he needed a haircut badly and he wasn't achieving much sitting here fuming about the faithlessness of Caroline. At five o'clock, Suzie brought him in some letters to sign. He signed them, then threw on his jacket as he passed back the correspondence folder to his secretary and wished her good night.

He strode down to the open air car park, one of the few remaining sites as property developers had been throwing up more and more office blocks every year, and climbed into a Bentley limousine. He pressed a button to roll open the roof of the ice-blue convertible (on loan from Lawrence Back Motors, a smart Berkshire garage owned by a friend of Martin Reese who paid for the occasional PR work by Cable Publicity with a week's loan here and there of a limousine). In fact, Martin had planned to drive his prospective new client down to the races that afternoon in the Bentley, but the man concerned had just taken possession of a new car himself the previous week and insisted that he ferry Martin and Dave Green to Hurst Park in his own vehicle.

'Nice car, Mr Belling,' said the elderly car park attendant as he handed Martin his sixpence change from the ten shilling note Ivor had given him with his ticket.

'Too big for London, Bob,' said Ivor briskly. 'The firm wanted me to have this but I said no; a Mini's the car for London traffic, nips in and out of the jams much quicker than this monster.'

'I'd have taken it off your hands if you've no further use for it, but I 'aven't got a garage and I wouldn't want to keep it in the street or the neighbours would think I was showing off.'

'Just as well then that it's going back tomorrow night,' Ivor said as he swung up the exit ramp into Proctor Street. 'Save me a good spot tomorrow, Bob. I'll probably be in nice and early.'

Ivor waited patiently for a driver to let him squeeze into a lane of traffic and he reflected that there was one advantage over driving a Mini – people were far more likely to give way and let you in. But the sight of a Rolls or a Bentley often raised hackles and a large number of drivers (including himself) usually decided that they would be damned if they would make way for some rich bastard! However, the journey to Mayfair was not too horrific and just twenty-five yards away from Shimmy's salon, Ivor manoeuvred the gleaming limousine into a parking space just vacated by an MG sports car which suddenly shot out in front of him. He fumbled in his pocket and brought out the solitary sixpence which Bob, the car park attendant, had just given him. Shit, that won't give me enough time on the meter, he muttered to himself, but then he glanced up and saw that the MG driver had left more than half an hour's free time on the clock so that the sixpence would take him up to the magic half past six when meter parking became free of charge. A free meter in the heart of the West End and with unexpired free time on it, to boot!

Perhaps my luck is turning, thought Ivor as he glanced at his watch and walked into Shimmy's exactly on time for his appointment. He was greeted by a dazzling smile from the gorgeous blonde receptionist who was wearing a skin-tight white shirt through which Ivor could see the dark outlines of her thrusting nipples, and she had a ribbon around her hair which flowed gently over her shoulders. 'Good evening, Mr Belling, thank you very much for getting here on time. Shimmy is just finishing off his client. Can I get you a coffee whilst you wait for a few minutes?'

'Thank you very much,' said Ivor, taking in the girl's slim figure which was accentuated by a wide black belt around her waist and a tiny pink mini-skirt which barely covered her mound when she stood up. He noticed a gold badge on her shirt with her name printed upon it and when she asked him how he wanted his coffee he said easily: 'White with one sugar, please, Erica.'

She brought him the coffee and sat down next to him, smoothing down her tiny skirt provocatively along her upper thighs as he took the mug from her. 'Is this your first time at Shimmy's?' she asked and Ivor nodded as he sipped his coffee. 'Yes, I didn't think I'd seen you here before,' she said. 'I'm sure I would have remembered it if I had.'

'Go on, I bet you say that to all the guys,' joshed Ivor, and she lightly slapped his upper arm as she giggled and added: 'No I don't, honest. I've been here six months and you do meet some nice men in this job, but you also meet some creeps, believe me. I'll tell you who's really sweet, though, and that's Ruff Trayde, the pop singer. He comes in every month for a haircut and he has a sun-bed treatment as well. Would you like to try it? It tones the skin beautifully as well as giving you a nice tan, and if you like you can also have a massage, which most men find very relaxing.'

'I bet they do if the masseuse looks anything like you,' said Ivor with a roguish smile, and Erica giggled again. 'I don't know about that. You'd best ask Claire who's in charge of that department. Claire's a fully-trained masseuse, though she's teaching me how to give a good massage as I'd prefer to work as her assistant than be stuck here all day on the reception desk.

'That's Claire over there,' she added, pointing at another sleek blonde girl dressed in a white nurse's uniform who suddenly appeared from behind a blue curtain. 'She looks a little like me, doesn't she? Some people think we're sisters.'

'And are you?' prompted Ivor, but Erica shook her head. 'No, we're not related, though we are good friends. Claire and I live near each other and we often come and go from work together.'

There was a brief silence and then Ivor said: 'You're a good salesgirl, Erica. Is Claire free to give me a massage after Shimmy's cut my hair? I've had a rotten day and could do with something to make me feel bright and breezy again.'

Erica bit her lip and said: 'Oh dear, I hope you don't

think I was trying to pressurise you. It so happens that Claire and I are going to the cinema tonight so I don't know whether she'll have time. Hold on a minute and I'll ask her.'

She stood up and ran over to the other girl. After a brief consultation she came back and said: 'Fine, Mr Belling, Claire will squeeze you in.'

'That sounds super,' said Ivor suggestively. 'And I've absolutely no objections whatsoever if you want to come in and help Claire out as you watch her do her stuff.'

She looked at him with a mischievous glint in her bright blue eyes. 'Maybe I will at that, Mr Belling,' she said softly and Ivor winked at her.

'The name's Ivor,' he murmured as a tall Mediterranean man dressed in an open-necked silk dress shirt and tight blue trousers approached them. 'Is this gentleman my next appointment?' he asked Erica in slightly accented English.

'Yes, this is Mr Belling, it's his first visit, Shimmy,' said Erica, positioning herself neatly behind Ivor to relieve him of his jacket.

'Ah, good, I hope this will be the first of many,' said Shimmy as he escorted Ivor through a door to the men's salon which was beautifully tiled with black and white panels, and Ivor sat in a state of the art chair which Shimmy adjusted to the contours of Ivor's back. This was a million miles away from Archie's Hairdressers in Broadhurst Gardens, West Hampstead, said Ivor to himself as Shimmy bustled around him and said that a girl would first wash his hair whilst he decided on which style would best suit his new customer.

'Hey, I'm perfectly happy with how my hair looks now,' said Ivor anxiously. 'And to be honest, I'm not in the mood even to consider anything new. Incidentally, I've booked a turn on the sun-bed and a massage afterwards.'

Shimmy looked disappointed but said: 'Well, your hair looks in fair shape, I must admit, but next time perhaps you'll let me suggest something different for you.'

18

After another extraordinarily pretty Eurasian girl had washed his hair, Shimmy asked Ivor if anyone had recommended him to the salon. 'Yes, a business colleague of mine named Brian Lipman,' said Ivor and Shimmy chuckled. 'Good old Brian. Nice chap, isn't he? David Bailey told me the other day that Brian's quite highly regarded in the trade. Here, you're not connected with Cable Publicity, by any chance?'

Ivor was amused to notice that the slight foreign accent had now disappeared into broad South London Cockney as he revealed his identity. 'I'm a director of Cable,' he said with a small smile. 'And besides Brian Lipman, I understand that our businesses name someone else in common. One of our top clients is Ruff Trayde. Erica was just telling me that he's a frequent visitor here.'

'Sure, all the girls go mad about him,' said Shimmy and then glancing around him, he lowered his voice. 'Is it true though that he's a shirtlifter on the quiet? I must say, he's never actually made a play for any of my girls, though they'd all drop their knickers for him if he asked them to.'

Ivor waved away the idea with a flick of his fingers. 'It's terrible how that rumour got about. The truth of the matter is simply that Ruff's a religious boy who doesn't believe in sex before marriage,' he lied for the umpteenth time when asked about the young pop singer's sexual proclivities.

This seemed to satisfy Shimmy who finished cutting Ivor's hair with a further stream of gossip about various showbiz stars. He flashed a mirror around the back of Ivor's head to show him his handiwork. 'I've layered your hair nicely if I say so myself,' said Shimmy with satisfaction. 'Now you said you had an appointment with Claire, didn't you? Then let me show you into our massage parlour.'

He led Ivor through to a small room where Claire was sitting down reading a magazine. She jumped up as they entered and Shimmy said: 'Goodbye, Mr Belling. I do hope we'll see you again.'

'I'm sure you will,' assured Ivor as Claire motioned for him to sit down. 'Hello, Mr Belling, would you like to undress down to your underpants, whilst I get prepared. You can put your clothes on the hangers behind the door.'

'My name's Ivor,' he said in a friendly tone. 'Didn't Erica tell you?'

'Oh yes, of course she did. Sorry, I forgot. Okay, Ivor, I'll be back in five minutes and when I return I'd like to see you up on that table, lying on your tummy,' she said as she went out of the room and closed the door firmly behind her. Slowly he undressed and carefully folded his clothes, taking care to place his wallet in a zipped up inner pocket of his jacket. He clambered up onto the table and looked to his side to see the door open and Claire come back into the room.

But what a change in her clothing as well! For now the sexy, full-bosomed blonde was barefoot and wearing only the briefest blue bikini. Claire adjusted the straps of the halter that supported though hardly covered her creamy breasts which spilled out invitingly over the tops of the brassiere, and Ivor looked down to the tiny triangle of blue fabric between her legs. His cock began to swell menacingly and he adjusted his body to give his burgeoning shaft room to lie squashed between his belly and the treatment table.

'I suggest we begin with the sun-ray lamp,' said Claire briskly, handing him a pair of darkened spectacles. 'Pop these on, please. Now as it's your first time, I don't think you should spend more than fifteen minutes each side this evening. Then I'll give you a massage.'

'Fair enough,' said Ivor, putting on the glasses as he still lay face down whilst Claire switched on the sun-ray lamp. After a few minutes silence Ivor said: 'It's a bit boring and I can't read with these specs on – how about telling me a story?'

Claire laughed out loud and said: 'What, like Mother Goose or Little Red Riding Hood, you mean?'

'No, not exactly,' he grinned evilly. 'How about your swimsuit, though. I bet if those bikini bottoms could talk they would have an interesting tale or two, I'll be bound and much more exciting than Goosing Red Riding Hood or what have you.'

She laughed again and said: 'You're a cheeky one, Ivor Belling, and no mistake. Do you know, I've half a mind to tell you how I came to be wearing the damn things – they are part of a very expensive French bikini, by the way, made by Monsieur Edele of Paris.'

'Go on then,' urged Ivor, settling himself down on the sun-bed. 'And if you like I'll tell you how I came to be wearing these boxer shorts.'

'It's a deal,' said Claire as she swept back her hair and switched on the machine. She sat down on a chair by the sun-bed and said: 'Well, I won't beat about the bush. We get some very attractive men in here and quite a few ask Erica, me and the other girls for a date. Sometimes we say yes, sometimes we say no, but of course we don't mind a bit of flirting so long as they don't go over the top.'

'*Quae dant, quaeque negant, gaudent tamen esse rogatae*,' murmured Ivor, remembering his classical studies at school, and when Claire looked blankly at him he translated: 'Whether they give or refuse, women are glad to have been asked.'

'Who said that?' she asked curiously.'

'A Roman poet named Ovid about two thousand years ago, so it seems that human nature hasn't changed all that much.'

Claire looked impressed and she drew up her chair closer to the bed. 'No, I don't suppose it has – anyway, about three months ago this gorgeous guy called Julian came into the salon. He was about twenty-five, good-looking and really hunky. When Erica brought him in here, he said that this was his first visit to the salon and that the reason he had booked an appointment was that he had strained some muscles in his back playing football and that his friend had recommended he tried a massage from one of the girls at Shimmy's salon.

'"What's your friend's name?" I asked and he said: "Tony Mulliken."'

Ivor looked up in astonishment. 'Tony Mulliken? Do you mean Ruff Trayde's personal manager? Bloody hell, it's a small world – I know Tony very well because my firm does a lot of publicity work for the Mackswell Group who own Ruff and a whole stable of pop stars. Of course, Shimmy told me that Ruff comes here regularly so Tony would have to as well as he hardly ever leaves Ruff's side. He's got an eye for the girls, has Tony, but he's a very nice lad.'

Claire nodded her head in agreement. 'He *is* a nice chap and you're right, he does have an eye for the girls. He and Natasha, the Eurasian girl you probably saw at the front of the shop, had a bit of a fling a few months ago, which is all over now, but they're still good friends. Is it true though about Ruff, by the way? Is he really a woofter?'

'That's just a foul rumour put about by people who are jealous of Ruff's success,' said Ivor mechanically.

'Oh yeah? Well, why is it that he never even makes a pass at any girl?' demanded Claire. 'I've a friend who's a dancer and she's been in the chorus line twice when Ruff's been on *Sunday Night At The London Palladium*. He could have had who he liked but he just sat around reading the newspapers – though Tony Mulliken made up for him after the show. He took out two of the girls along with that new comedian Steve Williams and they had a great romp in Steve's hotel suite after the show.

'I'll bet they did,' agreed Ivor, who had been to some wild parties with Tony Mulliken in his time. 'But let's get back to poor old Julian and his bad back.'

She smiled and fleetingly let her fingertips stroke his thigh. 'Oh yes, I'd almost forgotten about him! Well, I told him to strip down to his pants and I went out to change. I shouldn't really tell you this, Ivor, but we don't have to wear bikinis, you know. It's just that if we think we're going to get oil on our clothes during a massage, we slip on swimming costumes instead.'

Ivor's eyes gleamed as he looked up lasciviously at the shapely, bikini-clad young blonde and said smoothly: 'And very understandable too! I just wonder why the oils should get smeared all over your clothes. However, I hope that I can guess the answer to that one!'

Claire looked crossly at him and replied: 'We don't charge more for the massage and there's no hanky-panky on offer, if that's what you're thinking. Sometimes, though, we simply feel like taking off our clothes. But I'll change back now if you prefer.'

'No, no, no,' said Ivor hastily.

'All right, then. Now do you want to hear this story or not?'

Wisely, Ivor said nothing more but nodded and lay back to listen to Claire who continued: 'When I came back dressed in a bikini, Julian was lying on his tummy, wearing nothing except a jockstrap so I could admire his naked lean buttocks. Now, I wasn't going to admit that like most girls, a man's tight little bottom really turns me on. So I decided to play it very cool and said: "What's the matter, have you run out of Y-fronts or are you just kinky?"

'He turned round and looked at me with a pained expression. "Tony Mulliken told me to change into a jockstrap for my visit because it allows you more freedom to massage me. Was he having me on, then?"

' "Yes, I'm afraid he was, but actually it's not such a bad idea," I said and pulled him back on his tummy and thought that Tony must also have told him about the swimming costumes because he didn't say a word about my having changed into a bikini. Anyway, I dipped my hands into the baby oil we use and began to smooth it into the skin of his back in long, slow, sensuous strokes.

' "M'mmm, how nice, how very, very nice," he sighed. "My muscles already feel so relaxed." His eyelids fluttered and in five minutes Julian was half asleep as I

23

continued to grease his back, all the way from his neck down to his bum cheeks. I began to rub the oil onto his buttocks and he purred with pleasure as I ran my palms over them. But when I moved my hands up towards the small of his back his whole body tensed and jerked upwards whilst he grunted with pain, and as I couldn't resist sliding my fingers underneath and giving his crotch a friendly squeeze I felt his massive erection. He gurgled again, but this time not from pain but from pleasure as I rolled the straps of his jockstrap over his rounded little bum and he lifted his body to let me finish the job and pull it down to his ankles.

'Julian turned over onto his back and revealed one of the biggest pricks I had ever seen. He must have had at least nine inches of hard, solid cock and my pussy began to moisten as I smeared some fresh oil over my hand and grasped hold of this huge throbbing monster, slicking my hand up and down the throbbing veiny shaft whilst Julian (who was nothing if not quick on the uptake) reached across and tugged down my bikini bottoms. I stepped out of them and let go of his cock for a moment to unhook my top which fell on the floor, leaving me absolutely naked. I grabbed a handful of tissues to wipe the oil off Julian's tool as I wanted to suck it but immediately after I had cleaned off the grease, before I could open my mouth, his gigantic cannon exploded and sent a fierce jet of jism shooting high into the air.

'At first I thought Julian might be one of those poor chaps who have this problem of coming too quickly, though these cocks wilt after giving out a gentle ooze and, unbelievably, Julian's cock was almost as rigid as before he'd spunked. I lay down beside him on the sun-bed and in a flash our arms and legs were entangled together as our mouths clamped together in a wet French kiss. Then he pulled away and whispered: "I want to taste your cunt, Claire."

'"Go on then," I urged as I lay down with my head on the pillow and athletically he moved between my legs and buried his face between my thighs. Oh God! When I felt his pointed, hot tongue lapping around my crack I quivered all over, especially when he parted my cunny lips with his hands and thrust his tongue up inside me as far as it would go. I adore being eaten but so few men really know how to lick pussy. Julian, though, was a master of the art. His tongue was hard, hot and slippery and he tongued me beautifully whilst his teeth nibbled gently on my clitty. I felt my climax coming and groaned loudly, holding his head still whilst I rubbed my hairy pussy all over his face, feeling his nose against my cheeks, then against my clitty as I pushed myself against him, smearing his face with cunny juice. I came in a series of huge, thrusting spasms as Julian clambered up onto his knees, his enormous circumcised dick standing up like a flagpole between his legs.

'"Gently does it," I advised as he guided his weapon to my eager cunt – but I need not have worried for Julian cleverly stroked his shaft all along my now soaking slit, lubricating his huge knob with my pussy juice. I just had to have it inside my cunny and I arched my hips off the bed to receive it. His cock went in, partly at first, and then the full length was buried deep inside my clinging, sopping quim.

'"Oh yes, yes, I'm right up your lovely cunt," he breathed and then he began to fuck me like crazy, his stiff cock pistoning squelchily up and down my love channel as its velvet lips opened and closed over his glistening shaft and I responded frantically, wrapping my legs around his waist. I wriggled my bum to better absorb his tool and somehow Julian managed to push in every inch inside me so that our pubic hairs were matted together as his balls banged against my bum cheeks.

'"Can I come inside you?" he panted and I told him that it would be okay as I was on the pill. "Yes, yes, go on Julian, fuck away, you randy, big-cocked boy," I replied and the bed shook as we fucked away frenetically. As his body jerked up and down, faster and faster, my orgasm came up on me far more quickly than usual. My cunt went into convulsions as Julian drenched my honeypot with a deluge of hot, sticky spunk and I clung on to him for dear life.

'When I came down to earth he laughed and said that I had screamed so loud that he was afraid that somebody would come running in! At last his cock now finally deflated, though still in my dripping cunny, and he slowly withdrew it. He knelt before me and I took hold of his gleaming prick as it hung there, still gleaming with our love juices, and leaned forward to plant a big kiss on his shining knob.

'He slipped on his clothes and I put my bikini back on. "How does your back feel now?" I asked and he grinned. "It's fine. I can't feel any pain at all. I'll have to get injured again to treat myself to another of your wonderful massages!"

'Well, to cut a long story short, we dated for a few weeks and I think it's fair to say that we both thought each other was the best fuck we'd had for a hell of a long time. But then Julian was sent to France by his firm and he's been living there for the last nine months. He sent me this bikini from Paris for my birthday a couple of weeks ago and I've been wearing it ever since as, to be honest, it reminds me of Julian and the great times we had together.'

Claire looked at her watch and said: 'Time to lie on your back, Ivor, and now you can tell me all about why you happen to be wearing your boxer shorts.'

Rather reluctantly Ivor turned over, unsuccessfully trying to hide the burgeoning erection which had developed whilst Claire was recounting her sexual adventure. His uncapped knob popped out of the slit of his shorts as Claire settled back in her chair. 'Ah yes, I said I'd tell you, didn't I?' he said reflectively. 'Well, the reason I'm wearing these shorts . . .' and she leaned forward as he paused dramatically before continuing: 'the reason that I'm wearing these shorts is . . .' Again he paused and Claire smiled and said: 'Oh come on now, there's no need to be embarrassed!'

Ivor returned her smile and went on: 'No, of course there isn't. Well, the fact of the matter is . . .' and then he finished in a rush: 'I bought them yesterday at Cecil Gee's and I wanted to try them on today to see if they were comfortable!'

Claire burst out laughing. 'You rotten cheat! Here am I telling you all about my sex life, thinking I'm going to hear a nice randy tale afterwards and that's all I get.'

'Let me make it up to you,' said Ivor, settling himself down on the pillow. 'Erica told me that you two girls were off to the pictures after work. So please allow me to take you both out for a quick bite of supper and on to the cinema. What did you want to see?'

'Oh, I was only joking,' she protested, but Ivor insisted that it would be his pleasure. 'To be honest, I was only planning to go home and sit in front of the TV. I'd much, much rather spend the evening with two gorgeous blondes!'

She looked at him doubtfully. 'Well, that's honest enough, I suppose. And I'd better tell you now that what happened with Julian was very much an exception to the rule. I don't want you thinking that you'd get any special favours, if you know what I mean.'

'I do know and I still would very much like to take you both out,' said Ivor steadily.

Claire looked at him again and then said: 'All right, then, hold on for a minute and I'll see what Erica has to say.' She rose and walked to the door. When she left the room Ivor hastily popped back his now flaccid tool inside his shorts. He only had to wait a couple of minutes before Claire returned. She shut the door carefully behind her and came back to sit beside him. 'I'm not sure, Ivor. Erica says it's okay as far as she's concerned but that two's company and three's a crowd and she wants to bow out. I don't want to let her down, so I think I might have to say no.'

'Send her in. Perhaps I can change her mind,' said Ivor promptly.

'Thanks, I'd appreciate it,' she said gratefully. 'It's not that I don't want to go out with you, Ivor, but I'd hate it if a girl ditched me just because she had the chance of a sudden date with a fella.'

'Quite right, I'd feel the same way if a mate let me down at the last minute because he could take out a ravishing girl like you. I'd also be very jealous!'

It didn't take too long for Ivor to persuade Erica to make up the threesome as he had suggested. He could have simply asked Claire for a future date, but Ivor correctly judged that he would be shown in a far better light if he pressed ahead with his original plan. Claire changed into her clothes whilst he finished his time on the sun-bed and, twenty minutes later, he walked out of Shimmy's a far happier man than when he had walked in, with a beautiful blonde hanging on each arm.

'Wow! A Bentley!' said Erica admiringly when they reached his car. 'It's only on loan,' he explained and went on: 'I don't often bring my car to work and the boss was going to use this one to ferry a prospective client to the races. As it happened, he didn't need to so I'll have the Bentley till the weekend.'

He unlocked the doors and Erica slid into the back seat. Claire sat in front with Ivor who then asked the girls to tell him where they wanted to go. 'The Academy in Oxford Street,' said Erica brightly. 'We fancied that new Swedish film *Elvira Madigan*. Have you heard about it?'

'Yes, I read a rave review in the papers. I'll pop the car in the Poland Street garage and we can have a nice pasta at Luigi's round the corner first,' said Ivor happily, as he had expected that the girls had wanted to see *Alfie* with Michael Caine which was probably the most popular film in the West End, and he'd seen it already at a press show as Cable Publicity were helping promote a young actress who had a very minor role.

The evening went well from the moment they sat down in Luigi's cheerful trattoria in Berwick Street. After wolfing down enormous plates of spaghetti bolognese washed down by a bottle of chianti, they sat enthralled by the film, a tender tale of a married army officer who runs off with a tightrope dancer and they finally commit suicide rather than part. 'What was the lovely background music? I'd really like to buy the record if there is one,' asked Claire as they made their way back to the car. 'Sure there is,' answered Ivor. 'It's the second movement of Mozart's Piano Concerto No 21 in C Major, and because of the film the record's become so popular that in New York it's in the Hit Parade!'

'I'm not surprised,' said Claire dreamily. 'I loved it. How about you, Erica?'

'Super, though I wish there had been a happy ending,' replied her friend, tossing back silky strands of light blonde hair from her face.

'The night is yet young,' said Ivor as he unlocked the car. 'How about some coffee? We could go to the Hilton or somewhere.'

'No thanks, I don't drink coffee,' said Erica, sinking back into the luxurious leather seat. 'But why don't we all go back to my place and I'll make you coffee whilst I have my camomile tea.'

'Sounds fine to me,' said Ivor looking anxiously towards Claire. 'Yes, if you like,' she agreed, adding: 'I only live two minutes' walk away, so you won't have another long journey.'

Fifteen minutes later Ivor swung the Bentley into a parking space outside the door of Erica's flat in a side street just off King's Road, Chelsea. They trooped in and Claire asked if Ginny, Erica's flatmate, was in yet. 'Ginny's in Manchester for a few days visiting her parents, so I've got the flat to myself,' she replied.

'Hey, are you okay, Ivor?' she enquired as she saw Ivor suddenly wince with pain.

He nodded and said: 'Yep, I'm fine. I just get these

twinges in my neck occasionally. I think I'll book a course of massages with Claire – that'll help one way or another.'

'By all means, but if you want to help yourself at the same time you should take up some exercises at home. You sit at a desk a lot of the time, don't you? Claire and I have taken up yoga and honestly, Ivor, you come away feeling really refreshed from a class.'

Ivor slipped off his jacket and squatted on the floor in the famous lotus position, straight-backed and cross-legged. 'Ouch! I can't keep this up for long! Yet I knew a girl once who practiced yoga and she told me that this was the ideal position for meditation.'

'She's absolutely right,' said Claire. 'It may look uncomfortable but the posture makes it difficult to fall over, even if you fall asleep!'

Erica giggled and added with a twinkle: 'Why don't we try some of our exercises after I've made your coffee. I'm sure that Ivor would like to see us do the Dog and Cat exercises and might even want to join in.'

Ivor scratched his head and then heaved himself up off the floor. 'I'm game to try most things,' he said, 'but I'm gasping for a drink, Erica, even your camomile tea.'

'Don't be rude, it's very good for the digestion,' she scolded as she went into the kitchen to put on the kettle. Claire switched on the record player and shuffled through a heap of LPs. She said: 'Ginny, Erica's flatmate, adores classical music. She won't mind if we play one of her records.

'You're the expert, Ivor, how about this one? Mendelssohn's Symphony No 4 in A Major. Will we like it?'

'I'm no expert but my parents are keen concert-goers and they introduced me to classical music when I was a kid, and truthfully I've loved it ever since,' said Ivor simply. 'And the answer's yes, I'm sure you'll love it. It's very exhilarating and romantic.'

'Then we'll give it a whirl – but I won't put it on till we're ready to show you our yoga exercises. Here, let me take your jacket and I'll put it away in the bedroom,' said Claire, which made Ivor's heart beat a little faster as he wondered whether this harboured an invitation to stay the night with these two gorgeous girls. His cock stirred at the thought but he banished the delicious fantasy from his mind as he hated being disappointed and it was foolish to imply anything more than politeness from Claire's remark. Still, he couldn't help hoping . . .

Erica came in with the coffee and her own brew and Ivor and the girls sat down to relax as the music of Mendelssohn filled the room. Despite himself, Ivor was starting to get horny as he looked across at Erica's large breasts which jiggled so invitingly inside her tight white blouse when she moved.

When the last strains of the music died away, Erica mentioned that she felt warm and went over to open a window, but Claire said she'd prefer it if Erica would not let in the cold night air. Ivor looked up sharply when she went on to say: 'Darling, if you're so hot, why not take off your shirt?'

Erica did not appear shocked by this suggestion and a sensual, eager look came over her face as she stood up and slowly unbuttoned her clinging blouse. Underneath, she wore a small lace bra over which her large, creamy breasts spilled so invitingly that Ivor's prick shot up into an instant stiffness. His breathing quickened even further when Erica added: 'What the heck, I might as well be really comfortable,' and proceeded to calmly unhook the bra, bending forward and slipping down the straps so as to let it flutter to the ground.

She glided gracefully over to the record player and glanced through the pile of records. Ivor's attention was now firmly fixed on her swollen strawberry nipples which were already erect, though from the corner of his eye he noticed Claire walk out of the room. He looked back towards Erica who had now found a record that appealed to her and the urgent, driving tones of Count Basie's band now replaced the mellow music of Mendelssohn. 'Do you like jazz, Ivor?' asked Erica as she sat on the arm of Ivor's chair and began to loosen his tie.

'Sure,' said Ivor thickly as he kicked off his shoes and tore open the buttons of his shirt. He stood up and Erica murmured: 'If we've travelled this far, we might as well continue to the terminus,' and she deftly unbuckled his belt and unzipped his fly. He returned the compliment by unzipping her skirt and they wriggled out of their garments until they faced each other, naked except for Ivor's boxer shorts and Erica's frilly pink panties. The luscious girl stretched and ran her hands all over her silken body, sliding the panties down her legs and stepping gracefully out of them. Then she put her arms around Ivor's neck and pressed herself closer to him. He was totally mesmerised by her goddess-like nude body and stood stock still as she broke her grip and moved her arms down to pull down his shorts and momentarily clasp his throbbing shaft in her hands.

'Do you think my breasts are too large, Ivor?' she said suddenly, and he replied with complete truthfulness that they were absolutely perfect for her body. This reply made her smile sexily and she led him to a sofa where they sat down and she guided his nervous lips to her firm, rounded bosoms. By now his cock was even harder than before and he slid his hand towards her soft pussy which was already damp with her sweet-smelling juices.

Erica threw back her head as he sucked hard on her raised-up nipples and moaned with joy as, ever so lightly, his fingertips traced the open, wet slit of her cunny, flicking the tiny erect clitty which was peeping out between her pussy lips.

'Wait a minute, let's do this properly,' she whispered and laid Ivor out on the sofa. Then she straddled him, facing his feet so that her cunt was inches away from his mouth when she leaned forward and began to kiss his stiff shaft which stood high in the air at right angles to his belly. Her pink tongue flashed out and teased the tip of his knob and then she opened her mouth wide to swallow as much of his prick as she could as Ivor arched his back upwards, Erica's teeth scraping the sensitive dome of his cock as she sucked her fleshy lollipop with gusto.

He looked up and placed his hands on her rounded buttocks as he watched the delicate slit of her cunny open and close as she moved her thighs. Drops of pussy juice splattered upon his cheeks as he pulled her down until the lovely crack was upon his mouth and he used his tongue to good effect, sliding it up and down the warm, wet crack, savouring the tangy taste and aroma as he thrust deep into her cunt. Then he found her excited, erect clitty and started to roll it between his lips. 'Ooooh!' she squealed as he sucked it into his mouth and she groaned with delight, rubbing her cunt against his mouth as she continued to lash her own tongue around his throbbing tool.

They continued with this classic *soixante neuf* until it was broken by Ivor who croaked out that he was about to come. At once Erica opened her mouth and released his glistening shaft and suddenly Ivor was aware that Claire had returned and was standing naked beside them. She took his hand and guided it to her drenched, silky blonde pussy as she massaged her uptilted breasts and Erica reversed her position so that she now faced Ivor whilst she straddled him. She grabbed his twitching tool and slowly lowered herself upon it, working it into her warm, soaked pussy.

She bounced happily up and down on Ivor's cock whilst his hands were busy squeezing her wonderful breasts and perky red nipples. Moving on his rod with athletic expertise, Erica now talked to Claire who was lying on the carpet, gently fingering her misty snatch with one hand and kneading her breasts with the other. 'He's filling me up with his big prick,' she gasped as she rocked to and fro on his throbbing stiffstander. 'I don't think his cock is as big as Ivor's friend, Tony Mulliken, but then whose is?'

'Size isn't everything – frankly, I often feel a bit sore after Tony's fucked me doggie-fashion,' replied Claire, diddling her pussy furiously.

Ivor tried desperately to keep Erica's clinging cunt from milking his swollen cock too fast as he looked across to watch Claire play with herself on the thick green carpet. He noticed that her eyes were fixed upon his cock slurping its way in and out of Erica's cunt. He felt Erica's hand on his sticky shaft and he saw her offer her cum-coated fingers to Claire, who eagerly lifted her head and licked them clean.

This drove Erica crazy and she told Ivor to keep his prick buried in her cunt as she bounced up and down at an ever faster pace until she screamed out: 'Yes! Yes! Yes! Empty your balls!' and the juices of her orgasm so lubricated her cunny walls that Ivor came just seconds later and her juicy cunt continued to hold and thrillingly squeeze his cock until he withdrew his drained shaft as Claire now brought herself off with an excited cry.

Erica eyed his flaccid prick and said: 'Claire, I'm sorry but I don't think Ivor will be able to fuck you until he has had a rest.'

'Not to worry,' said the tall blonde, scrambling to her feet. 'I think my pussy could do with a rest too so, while he recovers, why don't we show him some of our yoga exercises? I'm sure they will help get his cock back up very quickly.'

'M'm, that's not a bad idea,' agreed Erica, lifting herself off Ivor and joining Claire on the carpet. She turned back to Ivor and explained: 'You really must try yoga yourself, Ivor. You see, yoga involves creating postures intended to stretch and benefit the body, and it not only promotes flexibility and releases tension but also provides stamina and strength. Erica and I will show you two exercises connected with nature: the Cat and Dog positions.'

Ivor watched with interest as the two naked girls first showed him the Cat exercise, arching and hollowing their backs, though Ivor could hardly tear his eyes away from their two golden-haired pussies. His prick began to swell rapidly when the girls took up the Dog position, which involved stretching their arms forward and heaving their bare backsides in the air. He jumped off the sofa and brandishing his thick stiff cock in his hand, placed himself behind Claire and carefully parted her delicious rounded bum cheeks before sliding his tool in the cleft between them and directly into her tight, moist cunt. She waggled her bottom, keeping his prick firmly embedded inside her as she moved round until she was in front of Erica who twisted herself round to lie on her back, grabbing a cushion from the sofa to slide under her bum which was now slightly raised from the floor.

He slowly expelled a deep breath as Claire made her cunny channel nip and contract as he pistoned his rod in and out of her love box and a perfect frenzy of lust racked his body as she now lowered her head between Erica's long, slender legs and began licking and lapping at her sweet pussy that he had tongued only a few minutes before.

Erica soared into outer space and gasped out: 'Oh yes, yes! Eat my pussy, darling! Lick me out! I want your tongue inside me – don't stop, don't stop! Lick my clitty and I'll come all over your lips.' Her uninhibited words gave fresh impetus to the others who started to gyrate and the girls came several times before Ivor sent a tremendous flood of spunk flooding into Claire's cunt.

They collapsed into each other's arms and lay entangled for what seemed like hours. Claire broke the silence and said that she always enjoyed eating a pussy whilst she was being fucked. 'You've never tried it, have you, Erica?' she enquired, smoothing her hand over the other girl's flat tummy and letting her fingers curl around her silky pussy hair. 'I'm sure you'll find it as exciting as I do. Would you like to see for yourself what it's like?'

Erica nodded her head and the two girls looked across at Ivor who heroically managed to rise to the occasion and the two girls together licked and sucked his cock to maintain his erection whilst he lay on his back with his head resting on the cushion. Then Claire lay down beside him and Ivor moved up and over her as Erica took hold of his cock and slid his knob into Claire's sopping slit before moving over to straddle Claire's face, lowering her pussy to her anxious lips as she faced Ivor. He grasped hold of her trembling body and started to fuck Claire very tenderly so he could prop himself up on his elbows and nibble Erica's tantalisingly ripe, red nipples.

Sure enough, Claire's clever tonguing soon had Erica coming all over her face and she greedily gobbled up Erica's cum, smacking her lips as she swallowed the pungent juice as Ivor started to pump his raging prick harder and harder in and out of Claire's sodden blonde bush. Like a steel bolt, his cock rode thickly through the wet channel, separating the folds of gluey skin as she clamped her legs around his back and drummed her heels against his spine as he pounded into her at great speed until he shot a huge wad of hot, sticky spunk inside her as a final, gigantic spasm wracked their bodies and they tumbled back exhausted onto the carpet, although Erica still had the strength to climb over her friend and suck up the last remaining drops of milky sperm from the top of Ivor's now softening knob.

Later they retired to the bedroom where it was Ivor's turn to lie on his back whilst Erica rested her wet pussy on his mouth and Claire mounted his sore yet still hard cock. He licked and sucked Erica's delicious crack whilst she and Claire played with each other's breasts. Claire twisted her thighs so lasciviously around his prick that surprisingly, considering that he had spunked so many times already, Ivor came before the girls who were forced to finish themselves off. They fingered each other with renewed vigour and rubbed each other's nipples before finally taking up a *soixante neuf* position. This soon led to a climactic release with Erica getting Claire to come all over her face and she exploded into Claire's mouth shortly afterwards. Then they lay on the bed next to Ivor, drenched in each other's juices, slick with sweat as they fell into a deep sleep.

Ivor was the first to wake at around five-thirty in the morning. He tip-toed out into the bathroom and closed the door quietly behind him. After relieving his bursting bladder he showered and dried himself with the big pink bath towel which he carefully replaced over the radiator. He wrapped a smaller towel around his waist, opened the door and was startled to see Claire in front of him. 'Sorry, I didn't mean to make you jump,' she said softly. 'Erica's still fast asleep but I'd like to shower and get back home before going to work.'

'Me too,' whispered Ivor. 'I must change into fresh clothes and I've an important meeting at nine o'clock, but I don't like leaving without saying goodbye to Erica.'

'Well look, you pop into the kitchen and make us both a nice cup of tea while I have a quick shower,' she suggested, and Ivor readily agreed. Five minutes later they were sitting in the kitchen sipping mugs of hot, strong tea. Claire was also naked except for a towel twisted around her waist and, despite the exertions of the previous evening, Ivor was still excited enough by the sight of her pretty face, draped by shiny strands of long blonde hair and her pert, uptilted nude breasts topped by prominent tawny nipples of a darker hue than Erica's, to feel his penis swell slowly under the cover of his towel.

'How did you become a masseuse, Claire?' he asked idly, crossing his legs to try and deflate his burgeoning erection. 'Did you train at a college?'

'Not exactly,' she said, brushing back her hair from her face. 'If you really want to know, it all started when I was only seventeen years old. My father is a senior airline pilot and one summer he arranged for my mother and I to visit him in Singapore whilst he attended an international aviation conference as one of the British delegates. We stayed at a very posh hotel and one afternoon I picked up a leaflet in the lounge which advertised Chinese massage by a Mr Ho Ling Tong. I had nothing to do until the evening when I was going to a reception the Government was giving for the delegates, so I called him and within an hour we were in my bedroom and Mr Ho was unpacking a little bag of oils. He spoke excellent English and told me to undress and lie face down on the bed with only a towel over my hips.

'I was a bit worried at first but I gradually relaxed when he began massaging my back and I could see that he had no funny business in mind. However, I tensed up again when he removed the towel and started to knead my buttocks, and again when he tapped me to roll over, but I kept my eyes closed and told myself that he was a professional and that a nude girl spread-eagled in front of him was nothing new.'

'Oh dear, I'm afraid you were a little naive. I suppose that's when he began getting fresh,' sighed Ivor. 'Did you have a problem fighting him off?'

'No, I had no problem at all with Mr Ho,' Claire said with a smile. 'He continued to manipulate my muscles without touching my breasts or my pussy, yet I quickly became aware that I was being turned on in the most powerful fashion. It was as if my whole body was being bathed in tingling, warm waves of pleasure which were spreading out all over from my pussy. This marvellous sensation went on and on, and just as I was shuddering unbearably from this powerful feeling he lightly touched the tips of my nipples with the palms of his hands. I came immediately in a lovely, long surge and when I finally started to relax he began to stroke my inner thighs, back and forth, then moving between my pussy and my bum. Finally he tweaked my clitty and I came again, writhing wildly for goodness knows how long, for I had never experienced multiple orgasms before and I was literally out of my mind with pleasure.

'Finally, he stopped and wiped me off with a towel. I reached out for my purse and paid him and he slipped out of the room, leaving me drifting in a daze on the bed. I felt so randy that I would have even fucked the bell-boy if he had come in, but instead I had to wait till the party that evening when I met Mark Blumberg, a charming Israeli official of the El Al airline, and we balled the night away in his room.'

Ivor gulped down his tea and went over to the sink to wash out his mug. 'I'm off to Bonnie Scotland early next week, Claire, but I'll book an appointment with you as soon as I come back,' he promised. 'And I can't pretend that I haven't enjoyed Erica being with us!'

'You don't have to go back to Shimmy's, Ivor, it's not necessary.'

'I *want* to, Claire,' he emphasised and, looking at his watch, he added: 'I must get dressed and be on my way. If Erica doesn't wake up by the time I've gone, give her my love and a goodbye kiss from me.'

In fact, Claire had to perform these duties as Erica was still soundly asleep when Ivor closed the front door a few minutes before six o'clock. It was a bright September morning and he enjoyed the drive back to Hampstead through the almost deserted streets. He parked outside his new garden flat in Gayton Road and exchanged greetings with the milkman who had just rolled up in his electric float.

'Morning, Fred, glad I haven't missed you – could you leave an extra pint today, please?' he called out.

'Morning, Mr Belling, will do. You starting early or finishing late?'

'Just come back from a conference, and now I'm off again. It's okay for some who knock off after lunch.'

'I should say, and those who come back home with lipstick on their collars aren't doing too badly, either,' responded Fred spiritedly.

Ivor grinned as he opened his front door and waited for Fred to come and give him his two bottles. 'Public relations you work in, don't you, Mr Belling?' said the old milkman. 'Nice work if you can get it.'

There was time to wash, shave, change his clothes and wolf down his usual breakfast of cereal, toast, orange juice and tea before he was back behind the wheel of the Bentley, gunning his way back into town.

It was only half past eight when he approached the glass doors of Cable Publicity's offices and he was surprised to discover that someone must have already arrived before him and had taken in the milk because Judy, the receptionist and switchboard operator, who was usually the first in, rarely appeared much before nine o'clock. Whoever had come in before him had left the morning mail and the milk on Judy's desk and Ivor wondered who else had made an early start. Nice to know that we have some keen staff, said Ivor to himself, as he pushed open the door and strode down the corridor to his office.

The meeting about which he had told Claire was with Lawrence Back, the owner of the car showrooms from which Cable's managing director had borrowed the Bentley. Ivor had commissioned Craig Grey, their recently appointed director of market research, to come up with a clever idea for a survey which would help get Back's showrooms into the columns of the newspapers. The good-looking young man, who had previously worked for Tilers, a large advertising agency, had suggested finding out what colours of cars were most popular with successful businessmen and getting a psychologist to comment on the results. Ivor would then add a few words 'by Mr Lawrence Back, managing director of one of Britain's leading garages' and with luck, his client's name would appear in most of the papers and might even be mentioned on the local TV programme.

Ivor decided to walk through to the market research department and see if the report was ready. Craig must have been the early bird, he decided when he heard some faint noises coming out of the research director's office. However, the sounds emanating from Craig Grey's office were suspiciously familiar and were related to after-hours activities. Surely he can't be at it at this time of day, Ivor muttered, and without knocking, opened the door.

But his ears had not deceived him, for sitting in his chair with his eyes closed was Cable Publicity's research director with his trousers around his knees and Roberta, his pretty secretary, on her knees in front of him, her thrilling body completely naked, licking and sucking his huge prick like a woman possessed, with one hand clasped around his shaft and the other running backwards and forwards between his balls and buttocks.

'Faster! Deeper!' groaned Grey, and Roberta's head began to bob further up and down, opening her mouth wide to gulp down his throbbing tool until his body began to jerk frenziedly as he shot a tremendous fountain of spunk inside her mouth which overflowed from between her lips and dribbled down her chin.

They were still totally unaware of Ivor's presence, for the girl now positioned herself on her hands and knees on the carpet with her hips and chubby bum cheeks raised high in the air, and cheekily looked up at her boss and said: 'We've got time for a quick fuck if you're able to continue.'

Grey rose up from the chair and discarded his trousers and pants as he stepped forwards towards the randy girl. To his amazement, Ivor saw that the research director's glistening prick was still erect as he crouched behind her, nudged her knees apart and carefully guided his cock through the crevice between her bum cheeks into the warm, welcoming wetness of her cunt.

As soon as Grey's cock was safely sheathed inside her pulsating pussy, he began to fuck her at a fast pace, reaching round to fiddle with her large tawny nipples, holding them in thrall as he slewed his thick prick in and out of her sopping slit. Roberta's backside slapped sensuously against his muscular thighs as she slipped effortlessly into the rhythm of fucking which Grey had established, and he now increased the pace even further, forcefully pounding away as the randy teenager wriggled with delight. She reached behind and grabbed hold of his swinging ballsack as it cracked against her bottom and, sensing that she was waiting for him to climax, Grey croaked: 'Here it comes, I'm going to drench your puss, you little devil!' as his torso went rigid and he ejaculated his jets of jism into her seething crack. Roberta yelped with glee and she shivered all over as the pangs of her own orgasm swept like magic through her body, and Craig Grey now collapsed on top of his delighted secretary, who twisted her bottom lasciviously to draw out the last drains of milky sperm from her boss's now exhausted penis.

Ivor withdrew from the scene by stepping back and carefully closing the door. At first he was cross about the lusty pair using the office for their fun and games, even though (as far as he knew) they were not fucking in the firm's time! But the cleaner, Mrs Stoughton, would have a hard job removing the stains from the carpet and office romances had a nasty habit of turning sour. If Craig and Roberta fell out, then the odds were that Cable Publicity would be looking for a new secretary and these days a good, reliable girl was hard to find.

But his good humour was restored when Suzie brought him his mail and the first letter he opened was from Adrian Klein, a top executive of the international antique dealers Gewirtz and Gewirtz Inc. It was confirming Cable's appointment to handle the company's British publicity from the beginning of November, at the fees negotiated by Ivor and Martin Reese at a tough, six-hour presentation with Klein and Count Gewirtz himself, who had flown in from New York especially for the meeting.

'You look like the cat that got the cream,' observed Suzie as she brought him his tea in his Fulham F.C. mug.

Ivor passed the letter over to her. 'We pitched against three other top agencies and, frankly, I didn't think we were in with a chance. I even queried whether we should spend so much on the presentation – the artwork cost a pretty penny, I can tell you – but Martin insisted that we press on. Think negative and you'll get nowhere – but be positive and say you *can* do something and you've already set out on the road to success.

'Very true – a journey of a thousand miles begins with a single step,' said Suzie, placing the letter back on his desk.

'Who said that?' asked Ivor and Suzie shrugged: 'I don't know for sure, Ivor. It was the motto for last Thursday in my calendar! But I have an idea that it was Confucius.'

'Good old Confucius!' said Ivor, ruffling through the rest of his mail. 'Do you remember hearing all those silly sayings of Confucius at school? You know, like, "Confucius, he say no such thing as rape – woman in skirt runs faster than man with trousers down."'

'No, but you'd be surprised what jokes we used to tell each other at Roedean,' said Suzie with a saucy grin.

'I can imagine – but changing the subject, did Brian Lipman take your passport photographs last night?'

She coloured slightly and looked slightly embarrassed as she replied: 'Yes, I've got to pick up the prints later this morning.'

Ivor looked curiously at his pretty secretary. 'Everything all right, Suzie?' he said gently, looking straight into her large liquid eyes. 'Brian didn't hassle you in the studio, did he? He's a randy so-and-so, but I've never known him take advantage of any delicate situation and ask for repayment of favours. To be fair, that's not his style.'

Suzie shook her head. 'No, it wasn't Brian's fault, but between ourselves I had a little too much to drink with a friend before I went to the studio and I made a bit of a fool of myself there.'

'Well, we all do that at some time, don't we,' Ivor said comfortingly. 'Look, I have to go into a meeting in five minutes, but after you've picked up your passport photographs and finished typing out those reports I left on your desk, I'll buy you a sandwich at Yummies and – if you would like to – you can tell me what's on your mind. Anything you say will go no further, of course.'

She looked at him gratefully and accepted the invitation. 'Good, I'll see you later,' he said, rising from the desk with the Back Motors file under his arm and added:

'I'll be in the boardroom for an hour or so with Mr Back and Craig Grey, Suzie. Don't interrupt the meeting unless it's really urgent.'

Craig Grey was already sitting at the round, marble-topped table when Ivor entered the richly furnished boardroom. 'You're nice and punctual,' commented Ivor and was unable to resist asking Grey: 'Were you here early this morning, Craig?'

'Yes, I came in at about half past eight,' he replied.

Indeed you did, and you came again at about quarter to nine and a few minutes after that, thought Ivor as he sat down at the head of the table. Mr Back arrived five minutes later and declined the offer of tea or coffee. 'I haven't too long, boys. There's an auction of vintage cars at Farnborough at lunchtime so make it nice and snappy, eh?' he said, taking some papers out of his briefcase.

Craig Grey took the floor and cleared his throat. 'Okay, Mr Back. Well, we've established that colour preference exerts a powerful influence over the way others see us. I've got a distinguished psychologist, Professor Garry Horne of London University, to interpret the results of our survey.

'Now the most popular colour for up and coming young executives –'

'– is red,' chimed in Mr Back.

'Quite right, sir. Now people whose favourite colour is red tend to be gregarious but need to stay in control of a given situation. The colour itself is associated in people's minds with excitement, but business psychologists would say that those executives who choose red cars are impulsive, ambitious, individualistic and ruthless.'

'I think that's the best line to push,' said Ivor decisively. 'What the colour of your car says about you to your boss. How about the colour of my car, Craig?'

'It's green, isn't it? Well, according to Professor Horne, this denotes a cautious nature with a strong sense of duty, but that you're more interested in your family than your career.'

44

'I'd better make sure Martin Reese never sees this survey, then!' laughed Ivor, turning towards Mr Back. 'Just as well I didn't choose the colour myself, Lawrence, but simply bought the only MGB GT you had in stock. If I'd had a choice, I think I would have chosen black.'

Craig Grey leafed through the report and commented: 'Ah, well now, interestingly enough, this shows that you crave power, are success oriented and single-minded in your determination to achieve it. And Professor Horne also comments that you probably hold strong opinions and that the keynote of your life is a refined elegance!'

'Hold on a minute, how about your car, Craig?' demanded Ivor. 'You run a silver Humber if I remember correctly.'

The research director grinned and said: 'I checked that colour first, of course. It shows that I'm mechanically minded but that I shy away from any physical work. I'm very conscious of status and want to be admired. The plus point is that it shows I have a strong sense of duty, though I may be somewhat too rigid in my outlook.'

Is that so? Well, your John Thomas can't be too rigid for Roberta, thought Ivor as he said: 'I suppose blue was a favoured colour.'

'I'm glad you mentioned blue,' said Grey, leaning back in his chair. 'This was the most popular colour after red, and you may be surprised to learn that this colour denotes insecurity – the deeper the shade the less confident the person feels. Someone who chooses blue will be warm, caring and sensitive and can be trusted to keep a confidence, but though he may be a conscientious worker, he is too concerned with worrying about what other people might think.'

Mr Back snorted and said: 'It all sounds a bit airy-fairy to me. My car happens to be blue, and if you believe used car salesmen are sensitive and caring – jolly good luck to you! Anyhow, I must rush and I leave it to you, Ivor, to do the business. Quote me in whichever you want, so long as we get our plug in the papers.'

Ivor recounted the conversation to Suzie in Yummies as they munched through their gargantuan roast beef sandwiches. 'Two cokes, please Geraldine,' called out Ivor, and he said to Suzie with a laugh: 'We'll send the survey to the Press Association this evening, but put an embargo on it till 6.00p.m. tomorrow night. That way we'll get all the dailies and they'll have all day to work out their own angles. I'll ring Fred Newman on the *Sketch* and see if we can fix up a photo session at Lawrence Back's garage with a car and a couple of pretty girls.'

After Geraldine had brought over their drinks Suzie smiled and said: 'It's very good of you to try and cheer me up, Ivor. Honestly, I'm feeling a bit thoughtful about last night, but I'll get over it.'

'Tell me what happened,' he prompted her gently. 'Come on, a problem shared is a problem halved – you'll find that somewhere in the pages of your diary!'

Suzie sighed and twisted her fingers anxiously together as she said: 'Well, I would appreciate your advice, Ivor. It's just that I don't know how I can look Brian Lipman in the face again. You see, I had to pop into a party at the Three Bells round the corner. The girls were holding it for Dawn, Martin Reese's assistant, who's leaving us this week.'

'Oh yes, she's got an assistant executive job with Colman, Prentis and Varley, hasn't she?' said Ivor. 'But though Brian's studio is only fifty yards away from the Three Bells, let me guess, you suddenly looked at your watch and saw you were very late and you felt terribly guilty because Brian had told us how busy he was and was fitting you in as a favour. Is that what's bothering you?'

'No, I only wish it were just that – though I didn't get to the studio till ten past six. The trouble was that the party at the pub had started early and was in full swing when I got there and everyone was already slightly pissed by the time I arrived. Anyhow, the champagne was flowing like water and then some rotten sod spiked my drink with vodka and by the time I got to Brian's I felt quite merry.

He'd left the front door open for me with a note on it asking me to shut the door behind me. So I did as he said and went downstairs to the studio where he was already working on a lay-out for that new men's magazine – what's it called, *High Society* – and he was shooting some photos of this very attractive busty girl lying flat on her back on a tiger skin rug. All she was wearing were some earrings, a necklace, a black satin basque which she had pulled down to expose her breasts, and a pair of tiny black knickers.

'"Okay, Marilyn, open your legs a little wider and put your hand on your thigh as if you're stroking it," Brian cried out as his camera clicked and whirred. "Oh, hello, Suzie. Make yourself comfortable, we won't be too long, but Marilyn has another job tonight so I must finish this session before I take your piccies."

'"Great, that's nice, very nice," he added as Marilyn lifted her bottom and pulled the material of her knickers into a thin black line so as to show off the shape of her crotch.'

Ivor nodded sagely, for he guessed that the girl Suzie was talking about was the aptly named model Marilyn Letchmore who was known in the trade as an eager exhibitionist who loved to turn men's heads by wearing outrageously sexy clothes. When she had walked into his office one day the previous summer to audition for a job, she'd worn very tight jeans and from the way she had pulled the seam right up into her pussy it was obvious that she was nude underneath. Later, over a drink, she had told Ivor unblushingly that she cut a pair of jeans into shorts, cutting them so short that the sides of her pussy were visible, and that on the beach she always wore microscopic bikini panties so that her long slit always came right up to the top edge.

'I watched as he continued to photograph her,' Suzie continued with a wry smile, 'and slowly but surely she wriggled out of the basque and then slipped off her knickers until she was stark naked and was sliding a finger into her cunny, brushing her love lips and giggling: "How about this, Brian? Will this turn on the readers?"

'"I should say," he replied, mopping his brow as she moved a fingertip slowly up and down her slit, easing open her lips and playing with the fleshy little clitty. I could see that he was getting excited by the large swelling in his trousers and when Marilyn said lewdly: "Come on then, big boy, let's be having you!"

'Brian screwed the camera onto a tripod and attached a long cord with a rubber bulb at the end. Then he tore off his clothes and I could hardly keep my eyes away from his prick . . .'

Her voice faded and Ivor said encouragingly: 'Carry on, I'd love to hear what happened next! Brian Lipman's quite well endowed, isn't he?'

Suzie relaxed and giggled as she swigged down her cola. 'He is at that! I looked at his long, pink tool with its beautifully thick knob as he knelt down next to Marilyn, who curled her fingers round his shaft and cooed: "Don't wait, Brian, just put it in – I want to feel it . . ."

'He lowered himself slowly on top of her, his broad thighs forcing hers still wider apart, and when he began pushing his prick inside her, parting her squishy love lips, he started to squeeze the bulb of the camera attachment and there was a flurry of clicking as Marilyn hissed: "Now then, fuck me . . . plug my pussy with your fat cock . . . Ooooh!"

'Then they changed positions and she knelt on her hands and knees and cocked her bottom backwards as she reached between her legs and spread open her pussy lips. Brian scrambled up behind her and with his prick in his hand slipped it upwards until Marilyn gasped as he entered her.

'Softly at first Brian held on to her shoulders and began to pump fiercely to and fro, banging in and out of the crevice between her buttocks into her juicy cunt to the rhythm of *Paint It Black* by the Rolling Stones which was blaring from the radio on the floor. He was smacking his belly against her bum to the beat, reaching forwards to squeeze her breasts, and then he increased the pace to double time and he cried out as he shot inside her. But his shout was drowned out by the ARGH-ARGH-ARGH of Marilyn's frenzied climax. He held on to her as she quivered and quaked and stayed in her till she had ground to a halt before taking out his wet, gleaming shaft.'

'One of nature's gentlemen,' grinned Ivor as he leaned over the table and added quietly: 'So, you saw him screwing with Marilyn. If anyone should be embarrassed it's Brian Lipman and not you!' As he finished speaking, Suzie's face coloured up a deep shade of pink and Ivor quickly divined that the story had not yet ended and that Suzie had more to tell. 'Oh, you don't have to continue if you don't want to,' he added chivalrously, but the pretty girl took a deep breath before confirming his speculation that she had become involved with the randy photographer.

'I've started so I'll finish,' she continued, lowering her head as she dropped her voice. 'I was standing there, transfixed, when Marilyn saw me and shouted out: "Hello there, you must be Suzie! Brian's been telling me all about you. He's going to take your passport photographs, Suzie, but what he would really like to do is to shoot a set of you in the nude as you have such a perfect figure and are so pretty."

'"Thanks for the compliment," I laughed as she heaved herself up to her feet, wiped herself down with a towel and disappeared behind a curtain to change. Brian saw her off the premises and apologised for Marilyn's bluntness while he took out a bottle of white wine from the fridge. "Mind, she's not far wrong," he said, looking me up and down whilst we sipped the lovely chilled white wine. He slipped into his clothes as I continued drinking this wine, which I enjoyed so much that I thought it must be a very expensive French chateau-bottled vintage. So I was surprised when I looked at the label and saw that in fact the wine was called Procanico and underneath the name in Italian were some words which I read out: "*Denominazione Constrollata e Garantita* – what does that mean, Brian? Incidentally, this wine is absolutely super. Where does it come from?"

'"The island of Elba," he replied, pouring some more into my glass. "I was there in early spring taking some catalogue shots for next year's Erica Boleyn fashion group's mail order catalogue. I became friendly with some local people and when we left I was given a bottle one evening by Luciano, the owner of the hotel the girls and I were staying in. I liked the wine so much that I brought back three bottles and Luciano sent me a couple of bottles for my birthday last month. As to the *Denominazione* business, that's just the official designation given to the best Italian wines."

'Well, one thing led to another and when Brian heard that I hadn't yet had any supper he insisted on telephoning his friend, Paulo, at the Trattoria Mostro Azzuro in Museum Street, and a waiter came round in a taxi with two huge bowls of *fettucine* and a plate of fresh peaches for our dessert.

'To give Brian his due, I don't believe he planned any of this for a minute, and I'd be the first to admit that it takes two to tango, but I can hardly remember how I came to be sitting on the sofa with his arm around me. It was inevitable that we would kiss and as soon as our lips touched it was explosive – very, very urgent. Within a few minutes my skirt was bunched around my waist, my knickers were round my knees, my bra was tangled over my arm and my boobs were poking through my blouse.

'Perhaps I had drunk too much because Brian's voice seemed far away when he said: "Why don't we get out of these stupid clothes? I can't wait to see you nude, Suzie."

'As if in a hypnotic trance, I said nothing but stood up and peeled off my blouse and Brian stripped off whilst he watched me undress. For a moment I felt very exposed and vulnerable but then he crushed me in his arms and murmured: "God, I've been dreaming about this for months," and as we fell back on the sofa he kissed each of my nipples, making them stand up like two little red stalks.

'And then he whispered: "I must pay homage to your pussy," and he knelt down between my legs and kissed my slit as he grabbed my thin, well-moistened knickers from the floor and made a sheath with them round his forefinger. Then he delved accurately into my pussy, inserting his finger to the hilt, wriggling it about until the material of my panties were saturated by my love juice as I went into a mad frenzy at this sexy fondling.

'Then gradually he eased the soaking knickers out of the way and frigged me with his bare fingers until he pushed me down across the couch and I widened my legs in grateful anticipation, drawing up my knees to give his big cock easier access. He slid his prick into me and humped me to the most wonderful climax. However, Brian had managed to hold back so he turned me over and took me doggie-fashion, throwing his arms round my back so that he could scoop up my breasts in his hands and play with them as we fucked. I was so exhausted that I could only just keep my bottom in the air! But my cunny could squeeze his shaft tighter from that angle and this time he came off with a tremendous spray of spunk which filled my pussy to the brim.

'We rested for a while and then after we had dressed ourselves Brian actually shot the passport photographs! He ordered a Prestoncrest car to take me home as he had to work through until well after midnight, and I got home at about half past ten.'

She paused and a wide smile of satisfaction slowly spread across her face as Ivor said hoarsely: 'God Almighty, Suzie, you certainly know how to tell a randy story. I'm feeling all hot and bothered myself just listening to you!'

It was not difficult to see that the recounting of her adventure had also affected Suzie, whose eyes were now shining brightly as they exchanged heated glances across the table, and when Geraldine came across to take away their plates and glasses, Ivor dived in his pocket and pulled out a crumpled ten shilling note. 'Keep the change,' he muttered and he gasped as he felt Suzie's stockinged toes move up his leg.

Under the cover of the tablecloth she moved her foot upwards and twiddled her toes around the meaty bulge between his legs and soon she was stroking the stiff length of his shaft with her foot. Automatically, Ivor began grinding his groin against her and tried as best he could to look stoical, never letting on that his cock was threatening to burst out of the confines of his trousers.

'Let's go back to the office,' he said and they quickly left the sandwich bar to walk the two hundred yards back to Cable Publicity's headquarters. Within five minutes Ivor was locking the boardroom door behind them and they tore off their clothes until they stood naked, facing each other. He took the trembling girl into his arms and they kissed passionately. Suzie inhaled the smell of Ivor's expensive cologne and giggled as his abundant chest hair tickled her erect strawberry nipples.

He placed his hands on her creamy, rounded buttocks and pressed her towards him, crushing his cock between their bellies. Suzie reached down and wrapped her fingers around his pulsing shaft, gently peeling down the foreskin whilst his fingertips played around the edges of her sopping, hairy crack. She nibbled his ear and whispered: 'Take me doggie-fashion, Ivor. I'd not been fucked that way for yonks until last night, and I thoroughly enjoyed it.'

So he took her by the hand to the plush black Chesterfield sofa and she bent over the arm as Ivor positioned himself behind her. He smoothed his hands over her backside before pulling the cheeks apart, and she let out a tiny yelp as she felt his thick knob jiggle its way between her bum cheeks and force itself through her tingling cunny lips. He slowly slid his rampant rod into her and then withdrew all but an inch of his stiff, hard shaft before sliding it home again. He increased the tempo of his movements as he sensed Suzie's excitement rising, and then with a low grunt he slammed the entire length of his throbbing tool inside her so that his dark, mossy grove of pubic hair brushed sensuously against the cheeks of her bottom and she began to writhe like a crazed animal, shouting out 'I'm coming! I'm coming! Shoot your load now!' so loudly that Ivor was frightened that they would be overheard.

But he too was now past the point of no return and with a cry he spurted a fountain of hot, sticky spunk inside her tingling, delighted cunny. They came together in a gloriously frenzied climax and they tumbled down onto the soft leather of the sofa in a tangle of arms and legs, and this is where they stayed until they recovered from the lustful little orgy.

'Gosh, I don't know what's happening to me lately,' said Suzie with a small smile as they began to dress themselves. 'I've been feeling ever so randy over the last fortnight or so. You're not putting an aphrodisiac in the coffee, are you?'

'No, though what a good idea. I'll see if I can find something down the Charing Cross Road tomorrow whilst you're off to France with lucky young Warren,' he laughed, but he noticed a frown appear on Suzie's pretty face and he added quietly: 'Suzie, is everything okay between you and Warren? I mean, let's face it, you wouldn't have let Brian Lipman or myself fuck you if things were a hundred per cent between the pair of you.'

Suzie looked up at him and shrugged her shoulders. 'I don't suppose it could have been too difficult to work that one out,' she said heavily, sitting back on the couch. 'Though you're absolutely right, of course. I can trust you not to say anything, can't I, Ivor?'

'Of course you can, Suzie, and that goes for Brian Lipman, too. He won't say a word about what happened last night to a living soul. And that goes for anything you want to tell me about Warren.'

He sat down next to her and waited until she was ready to speak. 'Well, Warren does have a problem, but I can't get him to admit the fact and do something about it,' she said dully.

'Let me guess, he isn't always able to get it up,' Ivor suggested.

She shook her head. 'Not exactly. Warren can get it up, all right, but within seconds of starting to make love he climaxes. But he won't see that there's anything wrong and just says that he's highly sexed, and that the only trouble is his over-eagerness.'

'Well, that may well be, though the point is whether he suffers from a lack of ejaculatory control. How fast a man reaches his climax isn't as important as whether he has the ability to control when the orgasm takes place. I know a bit about all this because one of my oldest friends suffered from having too quick a trigger, and he went to see Sir Terence Cooney, a top Harley Street sex therapist, and since then he's had no trouble at all.'

'Now that's just what I want Warren to do,' said Suzie eagerly. 'What did the therapist recommend?'

'Well he told my friend Philip that the anxiety feeds on itself and once you accept that you need help, often a cure is very simple. A couple of stiff drinks can take the edge off anxiety, but the doctor said that you can often find your own cure. Tell Warren he has to work out a few little tricks to distract himself as he feels himself on the verge of spunking. He could try biting his lip, clenching his teeth or just thinking some very unsexy thoughts, like having tea with the Queen or thinking about whether Arsenal are going to beat the Spurs on Saturday.

'If these don't work, Warren could try one of these anaesthetic sprays on his prick before he begins. Philip tried one of these and it did the trick for him. Later, when he didn't need to use it and just relied on his natural techniques, Sir Harold told him that the spray he had been given was just a placebo of coloured water – but it worked, which just goes to show the power of the mind!

54

Anyhow, the point is that Philip's completely cured and he and his girlfriend are enjoying a great sex life. So tell Warren not to be so obstinate and go and seek help.

'God knows there's no shame about it,' finished Ivor with some passion, and Suzie leaned across and kissed his cheek. 'You *are* a kind man, Ivor. You should have been a doctor. You'd have had a marvellous bedside manner,' she said with feeling.

'Think nothing of it,' said Ivor modestly, returning her kiss. 'Come on now, we'd better get back to work,' but then, as he looked beyond her to the couch upon which they had just made love, his jaw dropped and he blurted out: 'Oh Christ, look at that sofa!'

Suzie turned round to follow his gaze. 'What's the matter?' she asked, puzzled by his sudden concern.

'Look at those marks on the Chesterfield! And I've just remembered that Tony Hammond's coming up here in twenty minutes with the managing director of Aspis's, an important prospective client in the fashion trade. It won't look very good if the guy sits down and finds his trousers covered in you-know-what!'

She burst out laughing and laid her hand on his arm. 'Don't worry, Ivor, I'll run downstairs and get the bottle of Perricks' Elixir from reception.'

It was his turn to look puzzled, and so Suzie explained that she had complained to Warren about marks left on her living room carpet after a particularly fierce bout of love-making, and that the next day he had produced with a flourish a small bottle of colourless, odourless liquid which he promised her would remove any stains. I bought a bottle for the office after Martin spilt coffee all down his suit one afternoon. 'It's expensive – seventeen and six for a small bottle – but it really does work.'

'Great! Please go down now and get it straight away. I'll call Tony and tell him not to come up here till I give him the nod,' said Ivor, who was very much relieved to hear that the problem was about to be solved.

Indeed, the afternoon passed smoothly as the stain

remover worked as brilliantly as Suzie had promised, and the meeting with Sandy Aspis went so well that Tony Hammond reported to Ivor afterwards that the account was almost in the bag. He was not particularly sorry when one of Back's Motors' employees came for the keys of the Bentley. It was a lovely car but he had often felt slightly uncomfortable driving it, as if he were wearing a borrowed Savile Row suit of clothes.

Ivor decided to stay late in the office and work on a couple of reports so that the hustle and bustle of the rush hour would have passed by the time he made his way to Holborn Underground station. So it was nearly seven o'clock when he bought an *Evening Standard* from the newspaper seller in Procter Street, who was just about to parcel up his unsold papers and go home when Ivor proferred the two large copper pennies for his last sale of the evening.

There was little news and he scanned the sports pages to see if there were further developments about Fulham's team for Saturday's home clash with Chelsea which he and Martin Reese planned to attend. He read with satisfaction that both Jim Langley and Johnny Haynes had recovered from injury and were expected to be named for the local derby.

Then his concentration was broken by the sound of angry hoots from the cars behind a red Mini, which had failed to move when the lights had turned green. A tanned, leggy girl with a mane of raven black hair jumped out of the Mini and walked to the car behind her, and when the driver wound down his window she said sweetly: 'Let's make a deal, you stupid berk. I'll press your horn if you'll start my car.'

Ivor laughed out loud and went across to the girl who was now sauntering back to her stranded vehicle. 'My I help you push the car across to the other side of the road?' he offered, and the girl looked at him with gratitude. 'Thank you kind sir, I was rapidly coming to the conclusion that the age of chivalry was dead,' she smiled.

'Dying perhaps, but not yet dead,' said Ivor as he settled his hands on the back window of the little car. 'Open the door and steer. It won't take a minute to get you out of everyone's way.'

Once the Mini was safely parked, Ivor opened the bonnet and looked inside to see if he could find out why the Mini's engine had stalled, although he would be the first to agree that he was no mechanic, and changing a tyre was about as far as his technical expertise would take him.

'I can't see anything wrong, though I would guess it might be a problem with the carburettor,' he said to the attractive girl who was bending over beside him, the neck of her white teeshirt pushed forward so that he could see that her uptilted brown breasts were uncovered by any brassiere. 'But I'm no expert, and you're very welcome to call the AA from my office.'

The girl gnawed her bottom lip and confessed that she wasn't a member of the Automobile Association. 'Not to worry,' said Ivor lightly. 'I am, so I'll call them for you. Let me jot down the number of your car.'

'Would you really? That is terribly good of you,' she said, flashing him a wide smile, her small white teeth sparkling against the golden tan of her face. Ivor looked again at the girl as she smoothed her hands over the sides of her tight white trousers.

'Stay here, I won't be too long,' he promised as he walked briskly back to the office. He returned five minutes later and said: 'You're in luck, someone'll be here in about thirty minutes. I'll have to stay with you, though, because the patrolman will want me to sign his timesheet. So why don't you lock the car up and then we can pop over the road to The Three Bells where I can buy you a quick drink.'

She looked hard at him for a moment and then relaxed, saying with a cheeky grin: 'Why not indeed – but I insist that I buy the drinks, Sir Galahad, after all the sterling work you've put in on my behalf.'

'I'm no male chauvinist,' Ivor responded quickly. 'But please let me hold your arm whilst we cross the road. I'm scared of all this traffic.'

The pub was almost empty and after she had bought a glass of white wine for Ivor and an orange juice for herself, they sat down by the window so that they could keep an eye out for the AA patrol. Ivor introduced himself and the girl said: 'Pleased to meet you, Ivor Belling. My name's Guiletta Headley.'

'Guiletta? *Sei Italiano? Di dove sei?*'

'Frinton-on-Sea,' she laughed, nodding appreciatively at his fluent, sound Italian. 'My dad's Italian but my mum comes from Peckham. You've got a good accent. Did you learn Italian at school?'

'No, not a word, but I spent five weeks in Riccione one summer vacation when I was at college and I picked up quite a bit. It's a lovely language, isn't it? I suppose you're bi-lingual.'

Guiletta shook her head. 'No, 'fraid not, although I can make myself understood well enough when I visit Dad's family back in Amalfi. I don't get much practice, though, as there isn't much call for Italian speakers in Frinton-on-Sea.'

Ivor grinned and decided to risk teasing her. 'I don't suppose there is. Frinton's such a terribly snooty resort. They don't have cream crackers on the table, do they, but crème de crackers instead.'

She returned his grin and said: 'Something like that – I suppose you'll now tell me the old story of the young bride from Frinton.'

He looked puzzled and said: 'No, I don't know that one, Guiletta.'

'Julie,' she said, looking him straight in the eyes. 'My friends call me Julie. Well, she undressed on the wedding night – took everything off except her gloves and her husband says, "Darling, why are you leaving your gloves on?" and she replies: "Well, mummy says I might have to touch the beastly thing!"

'I must remember that one,' Ivor chuckled. 'I know a chap, he's a photographer actually, whose studio is just round the corner. He's always got a good joke to tell me – but my trouble is that I can never remember any of them.'

Julie looked at him closely. 'You wouldn't be talking about Brian Lipman, by any chance?' she asked.

'Yes, I am – don't tell me you know him. What a coincidence!'

'Of course I do, and what's more I've just come from his studio. We've been working on some shots for next year's West of England Tourist Board brochure. Rather than take a chance with the weather, Brian's taken some great indoor shots of me in my swimsuit holding a beachball against a white background, and he'll merge them with a nice shot of Torquay with the sun shining.'

'Best way to do it. I hope they're using colour so we'll see your lovely tan,' said Ivor sincerely, adding: 'I bet you didn't get that in Torquay.'

'No, I've only been back a week after a month with my uncle in Capri. He keeps a restaurant there and I was helping out, working as a waitress in the evenings. But I had plenty of time during the day to lounge around doing nothing in the sun.'

He sighed and said. 'What a wonderful way to pass the time. Still, I bet the Italian lads were buzzing round you like bees round a honey pot.'

'They aren't too difficult to handle,' she said cheerfully. 'Especially if you can tell them to shove off in their own language. Italian boys are so vain that when they're rejected, at first, they can hardly believe you don't want to be chatted up. But once it sinks in that you're not interested they toss their heads and walk off, putting on an act of being mortally affronted and that, anyhow, you weren't worth their attention in the first place!'

They chatted easily and Ivor soon established that Julie was a successful fashion model on the books of Leon Goldstone's Churchmill agency. She was seldom without work, although he winkled out of her without too much difficulty the fact that she had given up her career eight months before when she had swept head over heels into a passionate relationship with a Greek millionaire she had met during a shoot in Crete. She later went to live with him, but the stormy relationship finally ended some six weeks ago and she had returned to live in London and was finding life rather tough.

'You know what they say, Ivor,' she explained. 'Out of sight, out of mind. I was doing well before I met Takis, but I dropped out of sight for over six months and new girls have now come in and Leon has to work hard getting me enough jobs to keep himself in the style to which he has become accustomed.'

'Perhaps I can help there,' Ivor began, but he was interrupted by Julie pointing her finger to her car. 'Oh great, the AA man is here.'

They rushed back to her car and it took only a few seconds for the patrolman to establish that the simple problem was that the battery was as flat as a pancake. 'I had trouble starting the car this morning,' confessed Julie. 'Two guys passing by pushed me down the road till I got started.'

'Well, you're in luck because I've got a new battery for a Mini in the van,' said the helpful mechanic and fixed it in for the grateful girl. Ivor signed the bill with a flourish and Julie said: 'I don't have my cheque book with me, but if you give me your address, I'll pop a cheque in the post first thing tomorrow.'

He looked at her steadily and said with a tiny smile playing about his lips. 'I've a much better idea, Julie. Where do you live?'

'I'm sharing a flat in Compayne Gardens, West Hampstead with my cousin Gwyn from Wales who's just come up to London.'

Ivor spread out his hands. 'My God, that settles it. It can only be fate that we've met like this, Julie Headley. If you lived anywhere near my way I was going to ask you for a lift home and then, if you were free, ask you out for a meal. Well, you could hardly be closer as I live on Fitzjohn's Avenue, just five minutes away. So may I have my lift and, more important, may I take you out for dinner tonight?'

'I'll drive you home with pleasure,' she said immediately, and then she paused. 'But as for dinner tonight, I don't think so, Ivor. I'm over Takis now but I'm not ready to meet any new men yet and anyhow, I promised I'd go to the pictures tonight with Gwyn.'

He looked at her with a mournful, hang-dog expression which he had found a great asset in gaining sympathy and getting his own way with women. To his immense satisfaction he saw her waver when he said: 'Oh *please*, I've had a dreadful day which suddenly lit up when you came along. Don't darken the horizon again, I beg you.'

'W-e-l-l, I suppose I could ask Gwyn to take Maureen, the girl in the flat downstairs instead. I know she's free this evening – she told me so when we met in the hallway this morning – and I'm pretty sure she likes Gwyn. He works as an editor with an academic publisher and he's a bit shy and needs a push in the right direction as far as girls are concerned.'

'Are you sure he likes girls, Julie?' said Ivor, brightening visibly as he could see that his wishes were to be granted. 'Don't get me wrong, but you know some of these highbrow publishing types have a reputation . . .'

His voice trailed off and though Julie was not offended, she shook her head. 'Oh no, Gwyn's not queer, far from it. Back in his little home town in Wales he was like a jack rabbit, but he doesn't know anyone in this big bad city and I don't think there are any girls in his office whom he fancies. So I suppose it would be a good deed to push him in Maureen's direction.'

'Of course it would,' cried Ivor happily. 'And now, *guidare, per favore* – but don't drive like an Italian, I want us to get to Hampstead in one piece!'

'Yes, I must admit that Italians are far better lovers

than drivers,' said Julie thoughtfully as she turned into Southampton Row and skilfully slid the small car between two lumbering buses as Ivor closed his eyes and counted silently from one to ten. 'That reminds me of the old story about a learned theologian who was asked by a student what was the difference between heaven and hell. "Oh, that's easy," he replied. "In heaven the English are the policemen, the French are the cooks, the Italians are the lovers, the Swiss look after the administration and the Germans are in charge of production.

'"In hell the English look after the meals, the French are in charge of administration, the Italians work on production and the police are all German!"'

Ivor chuckled and said: 'Tell you what, when we get to my flat, I'll wash up and book a table at Shackleton's, this new English restaurant in St John's Wood that won a rave review in the *Evening Standard*, and see if it gives the lie to that old canard about the English not being able to cook.'

She produced another of her heart-wrenching, flashing smiles as she said: 'Okay, it's a deal – but I'd like to change first, so would you pick me up, say, half an hour or so after I've dropped you off.'

Just over an hour later they were being ushered to their table by the suave head waiter at Shackleton's. The restaurant was almost full, even though the prices were sky high, and Ivor decided that the bill, which would leave him little change out of a tenner, would be on his next expenses sheet under the 'entertaining prospective clients' column. But the food was excellent and Ivor thoroughly enjoyed his Trout and Tuna Mousse followed by Fillets of Chicken in Lemon Sauce with New Potatoes and French beans rounded off by a delicious concoction of pastry shells with fruit and crême anglaise.

He poured out the last of the wine as the waiter brought a steaming hot pot of coffee and placed it on the table. 'Would you like a liqueur?' said Ivor politely. 'Cognac, drambuie, a Tia Maria, perhaps . . . ?'

'No thanks, and I don't want to sound like a killjoy, but I'd rather you didn't have one, either,' said Julie, reaching forward to let her fingers brush his hand. 'We had gin and tonics when we came in and then we polished off that lovely bottle of wine – and you're driving me home soon. Takis had a crash one evening after he'd been drinking and knocked over a motor-cyclist. Thank God the guy was only badly shaken and bruised, but it could have been a lot worse.'

Ivor did not argue but changed the subject. 'Do you miss life in Crete, Julie?' he asked.

'Not at all,' she replied promptly. 'Sure, Crete's lovely during the long summer when the sun is blazing down, but the winters can be pretty wretched with lots of rain and wind, and we were miles from anywhere and the road was often blocked by rocks which slip down from the hills. Also, when the tourists have all gone home it can get very lonely if you don't speak any Greek, as I found out when Takis had to leave me for nearly three weeks in February whilst he flew to Cyprus on business – it was no fun being holed up there with no radio, no television, no newspapers and by the time he came back I'd read every English book in the house three times over!'

'Well, I'm damned glad you came back,' Ivor declared and, in that instant, he suddenly knew that if they kissed they would finish the evening in bed together. His hand trembled as he lifted his glass of wine and drained it. There was a deep silence as Julie sipped her coffee and smiled at him over the rim of the cup, her dark, liquid eyes warm and inviting.

'You've made me change all my plans, Ivor,' she said suddenly, and he looked at her with a puzzled expression until she continued. 'I wasn't going to let myself come within twenty paces of any fanciable man, but now I'm not so sure.'

'I don't know what to say,' he stammered, taken aback by her frank and open words.

'Say nothing, but get the bill and we'll drive to your

place,' she advised. 'Then we'll go to bed and we can talk later.'

Ivor's heart began to pound as he called for the bill whilst Julie finished her coffee. He gulped down his coffee and fidgeted uncontrollably until the waiter came back with his bill. Normally, he always checked the bill, but now he was too eager to leave to bother, and with just a glance at the total he took two five pound notes and left them in the saucer. He stood up and went round to pull Julie's chair away from the table.

'Thank you for dinner, Ivor, it was really delicious,' she murmured, and they hurried out towards the car. The traffic was light but Ivor fought against the temptation to gun down Avenue Road, for he correctly judged that Julie was a nervous passenger and he had no wish to break the magic spell which was presently cocooning them into the promise of paradise.

Julie was as good as her word, for once inside Ivor's flat they threw off their coats and she let herself be guided into his bedroom. He put his arms around her, seeking her lips and, in a flash, her mouth was open, her tongue was lashing his, one hand running through his hair and the other pulling him towards her. He needed no further encouragement and, clasped together, they zig-zagged wildly towards the bed. As they rolled about on his soft mattress, his hands pressed her firm breasts and he undid her blouse and slipped his hand inside. As he suspected, Julie had not bothered with a bra and his hand met hot, supple flesh, her erect nipples making tantalising, hard islets on the satiny skin.

She sighed and groaned and ground her hips against him until he thought he might come in his trousers, and she must have sensed this from his anguished gasp, for she suddenly relaxed and lay passively as he bared her small but tiptilted breasts and rubbed the hard, rubbery nipples against the palms of his hands as they continued their fervent embrace. He now ran his hand along her thighs. She was wearing stockings and, as he discovered, a neat

64

suspender belt, but to his delight he found that Julie had dispensed with her panties. Perhaps she had discarded them when she went to the washroom in the restaurant, he thought, as his hand slipped off her bare thigh to where he expected to meet silk, but instead found himself touching her crisp pubic bush. His fingers explored the tender softness and, very soon, felt the first trickles of moisture dampen his skin.

Her hand now moved to his trouser belt which she unbuckled, and she unzipped his flies before pulling down his trousers. They continued undressing each other until Julie was naked and Ivor was wearing only his Y fronts. She wrestled them down over his hips and held his hard, throbbing tool, running her fingers along it, feeling its size – and then she leaned forward and washed the rounded knob with her tongue as she pressed his cock between her soft, warm hands. His shaft twitched violently as she sucked it in between her rich, red lips, but she found it difficult to keep the huge rod inside her mouth, so she switched to his hairy ballsack and began licking and kissing it as Ivor gurgled happily, and Julie went back to lapping his rock-hard shaft whilst running her fingers up and down the veiny pole.

Ivor panted a warning. 'I'm going to come, I can't stop!' he cried out as he tried to withdraw his pulsating prick, but Julie pulled him back and sucked his knob back inside her mouth, working her tongue all over the purple dome until, with a convulsive cry, he spurted a great gush of spunk which she gobbled down with evident enjoyment. She sucked and swallowed until she had milked his prick dry, and they fell back on the bed in each other's arms.

'Now it's my turn to be pleasured,' she announced after a couple of minutes, and Ivor leaned over her and tenderly kissed her on the lips. She responded by pushing her tongue deep inside his mouth and his cock began to stir as he pulled his face downwards to kiss the tanned skin of delicious, curvy spheres in his hands. Her arse was wet and open, spread like a flower, inviting him to plunge his prick inside her, but his cock was not yet ready for a further fray so he raised her bum cheeks even higher and tongued the tiny, wrinkled rear dimple and then moved along the secret pathway between her arsehole and cunt as he slid his face under her.

Unlike most of his male friends, Ivor enjoyed cunnilingus and his mouth fastened upon Julie's crack with practised expertise and she shivered with delight as she bucked and humped her quivering pussy into his face, trying to force his tongue deeper into her cunny channel. He found her clitty and probed at it with his teeth. 'Yes, yes, suck my clitty!' she panted as he licked and lapped round the erect little ball, whilst his hands roved over her breasts which sent her into fresh paroxysms of desire and she implored him to finish her off.

Fortunately, his penis had now recovered from their previous performance and had thickened up again to its previous iron-hard stiffness as he manoeuvred back up against her, spreading himself against the full length of her body, feeling the fleshy moons of her backside against the pit of his belly. Then he moved between her legs, nudging her knees further apart and, taking his pulsing prick in his hand, he capped and uncapped the ruby-coloured knob. Carefully, he guided his knob between the cheeks of her bum into her dripping cunny and started to fuck her, jerking his hips to and fro. He was kneeling now between her legs and bending forward so that his hairy chest brushed against her back. He reached under the gorgeous girl and cupped her breasts in his hands, holding them in a firm grip whilst he continued to pump fiercely in and out of her juicy pussy.

Julie's lush buttocks slapped arousingly against the tops of his thighs as he watched his cock see-saw out of her sopping cunt, above which the wrinkled brown rosebud of her arsehole quivered and winked with every stroke. Reaching behind her, Julie caressed his tight ballsack as she rocked to and fro, her head thrown back and thick strands of her jet black hair whipping from side to side.

She wiggled her bottom, working it round and round, her hips rotating to achieve the maximum penetration of Ivor's cock and then, with a wild yell, she threw back her head again in total abandon as she climaxed with a rush of passion which coursed through every fibre of her being. Seconds later Ivor's torso stiffened and, with an anguished cry, he managed one final thrust forwards, his balls banging against the back of Julie's thighs as his cock spurted spasm after spasm of hot sperm inside her. He felt himself racked by the force of his orgasm and he gave a last drawn-out moan before he collapsed upon Julie, his entire frame bathed in perspiration.

They fell into a deep sleep and when Ivor opened his eyes the sunlight was shining brightly through the window, and he realised that he had forgotten to close the curtains before he and Julie had thrashed around in their mad passion. No-one could see through into the bedroom, but he always drew the curtains as otherwise he wold invariably wake up with the dawn. He looked to his right and blinked with surprise to see that Julie was already awake, sitting bolt upright, motionless and with her hands clasped behind her head. He moved himself up and kissed the smooth insides of her arms, and she quivered as his tongue snaked briefly into her ear.

'Hi there, darling,' he said softly kissing her lightly on the cheek as he looked at his watch. 'You're an early riser; it's only five to six. Have you been up for long?'

'About half an hour. Sorry, I didn't mean to disturb you.'

'You didn't,' he assured her, cuddling her in his arms. 'I always wake up early if I forget to close the curtains and there's a strong morning light. How about joining me for a shower in a minute?'

'Sounds like a good idea,' she said, throwing back the bedclothes. 'Hey, not so fast,' Ivor protested with a smile. 'I had in mind something else first.'

Julie gave him a mischievous smile and threw herself backwards, her mane of dark hair spreading all over the white pillow. She insinuated a slim finger between the outer folds of her pussy and began to massage her clitoris, swaying her body sensually from side to side. Ivor licked his lips and plunged two of his own fingers into her moist, hairy pussy, tickling her cunny as she reached out and caressed his hot cock with delicate, feathery strokes until she slid upwards, putting a knee on each side of his body. Ivor responded by teasing her dripping pussy with the tip of his knob, rubbing it all along her slit before Julie lowered herself down on him so that his rigid penis was totally embedded inside her excited love channel.

'A-a-a-h!' gasped Ivor as she rode him like a jockey at Ascot, savagely pistoning herself down on his swollen shaft, eluding his flailing hands which at first tried to slow her down. Then Ivor caught the rhythm and started to thrust upwards in time with her downward plunges so well that Julie squealed happily as his prick rubbed itself against her clitty. Madly, they rocked together until, in a splendidly powerful release, he drenched her cunt with a deluge of frothy spunk as she orgasmed ecstatically and her love juices trickled down her thighs.

To his surprise, Ivor found that his cock was still stiff, so without taking his shaft out of her sopping crack, he pulled the quivering girl over onto her back and began to pump furiously in and out of her soaking cunny, watching her velvet pussy lips open and close over his wet, glistening prick. Their pubic hairs matted together as he lay still for a moment inside her in an aura of pure lust.

'Now then, lover,' muttered Julie wickedly. 'Oh yes, that's nice, keep on working that lovely big cock in and out of my cunt. Faster, faster now, I want you to spunk inside my sweet little pussy!'

The bed shook as he eagerly complied with her request, his thick, raging rod reaming out the furthest recesses of her throbbing cunny as they fucked at a frenetic pace. 'Y-e-s-, Y-e-s, Y-E-S! There it goes! Oooh, what a flood!'

she screamed as, almost dizzy from the effort, Ivor gave a hoarse cry and shot a second gush of sticky, hot cream as her body contorted with the force of her magnificent climax. He rolled off her and lay on his back, gasping for air as Julie wriggled forward and clamped her lips over his glistening but now flaccid prick, kissing it passionately as she licked up the coating of love juice from the deflated shaft.

Then she snuggled up next to him and put her arms around his neck and kissed his ear. 'Wowee! I haven't come like that –'

'Since last night!' interrupted Ivor with a grin.

She giggled and ran her fingers through his hair. 'Time for a five-minute cuddle?' she queried hopefully.

'I should say so, this is one of the times I love the best,' he remarked, and she pressed herself against him, but then she looked across at the bedside table. 'Ivor, don't you smoke after making love?'

'I don't think so, love, but then I've never really looked! No seriously, I gave up smoking a couple of years back. Didn't you read the doctors' report about how smoking leads to lung cancer?'

'Yes and I tried to give it up, but after Takis and I broke up I'm afraid I've started again,' she admitted. 'Still, if you don't have any fags here I can't very well smoke, can I? I don't think I've got any in my handbag.'

'No, please don't smoke, darling. To be honest, I can't bear the smell now I've chucked the habit. Sorry to sound so self-righteous, but my Uncle Mick died of lung cancer in his fifties last year and he'd be alive today if he hadn't puffed twenty a day for the last thirty years. I told the boss that I'd never work on a cigarette account and I'd probably leave if we even pitched for tobacco business.'

Julie looked at him with respect. 'A PR man with a conscience, m'mm? This is a very rare breed of flower indeed,' she teased as she stroked the dark, morning stubble on his cheek.

'So it deserves to be carefully nurtured, right?' grinned Ivor, wrapping his arms around the delicious girl. 'With tender, loving care?'

Their eyes met and she said softly: 'I think it would take a very special gardener to do the job properly.'

'I do too,' he whispered back. 'I wonder if I found one last night.'

They lay still for a moment until the spell was broken by the shrill ring of the alarm clock. With some relief, Ivor banged his fist down upon the bell and swung himself out of bed. 'Damn, I didn't realise how late it was. I'll run the bath whilst I shave,' he said hastily as he padded across to the bathroom. 'Unless you prefer a shower.'

Julie smiled ruefully. 'No, a bath's fine, Ivor. Call me when it's ready.'

By the time they had dressed, Ivor had remembered that he genuinely had to make an early appearance at the office to finalise plans for his journey to Scotland. Julie saw him look apprehensively at his watch and she said with a smile: 'Come on, Ivor, I'll put the kettle on. You shouldn't rush off without some breakfast inside you.'

He followed her into the kitchen and looked through the window to see a brisk wind winnow the first autumn harvest of leaves from the trees. Inside, the light bounced off the gleaming white Formica work surfaces and the two stainless steel sinks.'

'I like a man who keeps his kitchen clean,' said Julie as she filled the electric kettle. 'So many men who live on their own become very sloppy.'

'Mrs Waller must take most of the credit. She comes in twice a week and the place fairly sparkles after she's gone through it,' he confessed, passing the cereal bowls across to her.

'And I suppose she does your ironing and does the washing up which you leave piled up for her?'

'Not the washing up,' he protested. 'I've got one of these new Awaki Japanese dishwashers – actually, if you're interested in getting one, I can get it at less than wholesale for you as my company looks after their publicity.'

Julie rested her head in her hands as she placed her elbows on the table. 'My God, you've got it made, Ivor. So all you need is a regular bedmate and you're living the life of Riley.'

'Well, believe it or not, I don't have a procession of girls queueing for that job,' he countered, popping four slices of bread into the toaster. 'There's a carton of orange juice at the bottom of the fridge, and there's also grapefruit juice if you prefer it.'

After breakfast Ivor walked across and picked up the newspapers. 'I've got the *Guardian*, *Daily Express* and the *Daily Mirror*. We have all the papers at work but I like to flip through a few before I get to the office. Take your pick.'

'No thanks, Ivor, I must be going,' she said, gathering up the plates. 'If you want to get away I'll rinse them through before I go.'

A frown settled on Ivor's brow. 'Julie, this sounds awful, but I really must fly. Are you working today? You're very welcome to stay and leave when you want, but whatever you do –'

He stopped and she looked up at him. 'I'm listening, honest I am,' she said as he walked across to her and placed his hands on her shoulders and looked straight at her large, liquid eyes.

'Be here tonight when I get home, darling. I'll be back by seven at the latest,' he murmured as he kissed her firmly on the lips. 'And we can have dinner and do anything you like afterwards.'

She hesitated as he continued to look at her in silence. 'Ivor, I don't know. Perhaps it would be best if we finished things here and now whilst neither of us is committed.'

'You're still not committed by having dinner with me tonight, Julie, and I would hate to think that you passed fleetingly through my life without finding out whether you wanted to stay for a while and find out more about me. So please say yes, and I'll see you later.'

The lovely girl slowly nodded and said: 'Okay, I must be mad but, okay. Look, I have a job later this morning so if you'll wait two minutes I'll come with you. I must go back to my flat first and change, but I can give you a lift to Swiss Cottage station on the way. About tonight, though. Let me cook you dinner and we'll spend a quiet Friday evening at home. How does that sound?'

'Absolutely super.' He smiled broadly, giving her another kiss and hug. 'And I'll take up your offer of a lift if you won't be too long.'

They left the flat arm in arm and as Julie drove down the hill to the underground station she asked him what he would like to eat tonight. 'I'm easy,' he said lightly. 'I don't like shellfish or gooseberries, otherwise I'll happily tuck into anything.'

'Great, leave it to me. I'll be round at seven sharp. If there's any problem, here's my 'phone number or leave a message at the agency. I'll call you at Cable in the unlikely event that Leon has booked me in for a job which entails going to the Canary Islands this evening for a weekend shoot!'

She pulled in to the kerb and he kissed her goodbye before heaving himself out of the car. 'See you later,' he called and waved as she swung back into the hurly-burly of the morning traffic. He watched her manoeuvre the little car into the lane of traffic going north along Finchley Road, and then with a long drawn-out sigh he joined the throng of commuters making their way to work. It was going to be difficult to concentrate on work if the images of Julie's sensual, nude body were going to keep their place in the forefront of his mind.

Luckily the day passed relatively easily and, though Suzie left the office at lunchtime for her weekend with Warren in Paris, all the arrangements for his Scottish trip were firmed up by four o'clock when Martin Reese strolled into his office.

'Got your kilt packed for Sunday, Ivor? I wish I were going with you and Brian Lipman. You'll have a grand time up in Glasgow. Do you think we'll get some good coverage for the campaign? You know that those bastards from Brooke, Massey and Trewin are dying to get their hands on the Four Seasons account. So we need as many cuttings as possible.'

'Don't worry, Martin. I'm sure Mrs Rokeby won't let us down. You remember her? She's the breeder with the golden labradors who won Crufts two years ago who is prepared to swear by the stuff for two hundred pounds cash. All we need now is a little gimmick for the gentlemen of the press and we'll be well away.'

'And what's that going to be?'

'Brian's arranged for two girls dressed in not very much to walk a couple of the dogs down Sauchihall Street. The dogs'll have jackets with *Four Seasons* written on them and the girls'll be dishing out free samples to the passers-by.'

Martin pulled at his chin. 'Yes, not bad, not bad, but I'd feel happier if we had something a bit different which we know would make the *Glasgow Herald* and the Scottish editions of the nationals.'

'Well, we're seeing Mrs Rokeby on Monday, Martin. She also trains dogs for films and TV. I've spoken to her and she's promised to bring a hound to the press conference which will always eat the Four Seasons food first from a selection of bowls filled with other brands of dog food.'

'That's good, I like that, so long as it all goes to plan. Oh well, there's no point worrying about it now. Best of luck, mate, I think we'll need it.'

'So will Fulham tomorrow,' Ivor pointed out. 'Would you like me to pick you up as usual?'

'Sure, so long as we can make a quick get-away, as my dear wife booked tickets for a gala performance at Covent

Garden. It's costing me a fortune and you know how keen I am on opera. I'll sleep through the whole bloody performance if there's not too much shouting and screaming on stage.

'I doubt if I'll be able to close my eyes, though, as that fat Italian guy, Marchiano, is the great attraction.'

Ivor chuckled and wagged his finger. 'You're a real culture vulture, aren't you, boss? I know people who would pay you and Sally a hundred quid for your tickets tomorrow to hear Paulo Marchiano. He's amongst the greatest tenors in the world. I've read about tomorrow night's performance. It's *Turandot* by Puccini and honestly, Martin, there's some truly beautiful music and Marchiano has a superb voice.'

Martin shrugged his shoulders and said: 'All very well for you, old chap, but I don't even know what's going on and I don't understand Italian so it's all beyond me.'

'Well, opera's like Shakespeare, isn't it – you should never go without getting genned up on it first. Look, *Turandot* is a cruel Chinese Princess, and anyone who wants to marry her has to answer three riddles. If he fails, he gets bumped off. An exiled prince, Calaf, has a go and answers correctly. But Turandot is horrified as she hates foreigners, so Calaf says he does not want to take her by force and if she can find out his name by dawn, he'll die for her. She tortures a slave girl who kills herself rather than reveal Calaf's name, and this breaks down her pride and there's a happy ending.'

'Thank you, I'm sure that'll make all the difference,' said Martin heavily as he stood up. 'Though you're not wrong, Ivor. If you know what's happening on stage it does all make much more sense. Anyhow, more important, did you read in the paper this morning that Fulham will be at full strength? If Rodney Marsh is on song I reckon we can beat Chelsea.'

'I hope so, but they've got some bloody good players,' warned Ivor gloomily. 'Bonetti's a marvellous goal-keeper, Jim Langley'll find it tough against Bobby

Tambling and Barry Bridges, and I don't mind telling you that I certainly wouldn't like to be tackled by Ron Harris or Eddie McCreadie.'

'Maybe so, but I still fancy Fulham; they always play better against the best teams. Anyhow, pick me up a bit before two. There'll be a big crowd and it'll be difficult to park.'

'I will,' Ivor promised as his boss left the room, though his mind was filled more with thoughts about his evening with Julie than about the football match the next afternoon.

On his way home he stopped to buy a large bouquet of orange and yellow chrysanthemums which he placed in a vase in the kitchen when he arrived home just before half past six. He quickly showered and changed into the expensive casual shirt and trousers he'd treated himself to in the Harrods' sale, and was just combing his hair when the doorbell buzzed. 'Coming,' he sang out and opened the front door to see Julie standing there with a large carrier bag in each hand. He kissed her and grabbed the bags. 'Hey, it looks like you've bought enough for an army here,' he protested as he followed her into the kitchen and dumped the bags on the table whilst she slipped off her coat and hung it on the hook behind the door.

Julie caught sight of the chrysanthemums and gave Ivor one of her especially delicious wide smiles. 'For the cook?' she enquired, and he kissed her again as he said: 'I want you to take the flowers home with you so I didn't unwrap them. Now how can I help you? How about a glass of wine to start the ball rolling? Red or white?'

'White please, but let me unpack things first,' she said, slipping on an apron as Ivor opened the door of the refrigerator. Julie took out a bottle of Soave from one of her carrier bags and handed it to Ivor. 'And can you put this in the fridge whilst you're there.'

'Something very drinkable from the home country, but you shouldn't have bought wine as well as the food,' Ivor protested as she put a finger to his lips to still his complaint.

'It's going to be a very cosmopolitan meal, Ivor. Italian wine, Greek taramasalata with pitta bread for the hors d'oeuvres and chicken paprika from Hungary as the main course. I've cheated with the starter as I bought it from Marks and Spencer, but I'm cooking the chicken myself. I hope you like it.'

'I'm sure I will, but I don't think I've ever bought paprika in my life. Still, perhaps the little Indian shop in Belsize Park is still open,' said Ivor doubtfully. 'I'll pop down now and get some.'

'Silly boy, I never expected you to have any spices here except pepper and salt,' she said lightly, opening the second of her bags. 'I've brought everything I need – butter, onions, garlic, freshly ground black pepper, soured cream, chicken stock and rice. I've even brought my own casserole dish.'

He looked at her in astonishment. 'Gosh, it looks very complicated. Will it take very long to cook?'

'Not once I get started. I want to melt some butter, add some onions and garlic and fry the mixture on a very low heat for three quarters of an hour or so. Now, whilst I'm doing this you can lay the table.'

'I'd rather lay something else,' he said quickly and moved towards her, but Julie pointed a kitchen knife at his chest. 'Maybe I would, too, but the table comes first, darling. Go on, I'll be more receptive once I have things on the go.'

Obediently he gathered up the cutlery and went into the dining room to look for his best tablecloth. He placed two candles in the candlestick and rummaged around in the sideboard until he found the napkins which Mrs Waller had washed and ironed to a sparkling whiteness. When he had finished setting the table he went back in the kitchen and poured out two glasses of wine. He passed one to Julie and then sat down to watch her peel and chop up the onions.

'What was the job you did today?' he enquired as he sipped his drink.

'Nothing very exciting, just a few shots of the Aspis group's new spring range of dresses for next year.'

'Blow me down, it's a small world,' Ivor exclaimed. 'We're pitching for their PR work and made a presentation to Sandy Aspis in the office yesterday. With a bit of luck Cable will be handling their publicity soon, though my colleague Tony Hammond will be in charge of the account. He's looking after all the fashion accounts now, not that we've got that many, though we've been working for Ronnie Bloom swimwear for the last couple of years.'

'I did one assignment for Ronnie a couple of years back,' said Julie thoughtfully. 'He's a nice guy and the swimming costume was very stylish. But he's a bit of a lad as far as the girls are concerned, isn't he? He asked me and the other two girls to go out to his golf club and play a round with him. When we said that none of us had ever done more than try our hand on a putting green he said that didn't matter as he was more interested in showing us his five iron.'

'I'll bet he was,' said Ivor grimly. 'And quite a sight it is by all accounts, though I've never clapped eyes on it myself.'

'Well I didn't either,' Julie chuckled, 'though my friend Helen Newson has and she says it's quite impressive.'

'I'm not surprised. Ronnie gets enough practice, that's for sure,' said Ivor, sidling over to her and slipping his arm around her waist. 'Now how are you going here?'

She pointed to the oven. 'Take the pitta bread out, please, and we can have our starter. Then I'll come back and finish off preparing the chicken and we'll have another good half hour till it's ready to eat. Can you think of something to do whilst we're waiting?'

'Of course! I'll read aloud the first chapter of any of Charles Dickens' books to you,' suggested Ivor with a grin. 'I've the whole set here which I was given as prizes for English at school.'

'Oh, I couldn't possibly put you to such trouble,' she squealed as he swept her into his arms. 'I know, let's look out of the window and watch the grass growing.'

'I've an even better idea – come into the bedroom and watch something else growing!' he laughed as she vainly attempted to wriggle free. 'All right, all right, you've convinced me – but let's eat something first. I'm starving! Come on, take out the bread from the oven, there's a good boy.'

Reluctantly, he let her out of the bear-hug and she marched into the dining room carrying the bowl of taramasalata. 'I'll light the candles after I've brought in the pitta and opened the wine,' said Ivor, diving back into the kitchen. He returned with the bread and bottle of Soave and they settled back to enjoy their food. When they had finished, Julie added the chicken to the onion which had been frying in the casserole dish. She sprinkled paprika, salt and pepper and then covered the dish. 'We've got twenty minutes till I need to look at it again to see if I need to add a little chicken stock,' she commented as Ivor pinioned her arms to her sides.

Ivor affected the voice of a sergeant major, bellowing out: 'So I have your undivided attention for twenty, uninterrupted minutes? Then right about turn, quick march! One, two, one, two, one two,' as he guided her into the bedroom.

'Lord save me, am I to be ravished without so much as a by-your-leave?' she squawked as Ivor tore off his shirt and kicked off his shoes.

'I'm afraid so,' he replied regretfully. 'No, hang on a second,' and he reached behind her to pick up a notebook and ballpoint pen which were lying on his dressing table. He scribbled 'by your leave' on the open page, tore it out and solemnly gave it to the giggling girl. 'There you are, ma'am, one by your leave,' he announced with a flourish. 'It is yours to keep till the end of time.'

'Ah, well in that case let's not waste any more time and get on with the ravishing,' she said throatily, crossing her hands as she dropped them to her waist in order to pull her beige cashmere jumper over her head together with her slip in one fell swoop so that her proud, jutting breasts were immediately exposed. Ivor unbuckled his belt and sat on the bed as he rolled down his socks and Julie unzipped her skirt, letting it fall to the floor.

In a very few seconds Julie was totally naked and she moved swiftly to the bed and lay waiting for Ivor as he frantically unzipped his flies and sat on the bed to pull off his trousers and underpants. Once he was naked he stood over her, his hard, erect cock standing up high, almost against his belly, as he marvelled at her sensual beauty. He passed his tongue over his lips as he gazed down on her proud, jutting breasts capped by large strawberry nipples which were already standing out in anticipation of being licked and lapped, and her bushy triangle of silky dark hair looked more inviting than anything she could be preparing for their dinner. He laid himself down next to her and they smiled at each other before their bodies slammed together as he gathered her in his arms. She pulled his face towards hers and sank her pink tongue in his mouth whilst his hands moved across the soft curves of her breasts.

Julie grasped Ivor's swollen shaft and trembled all over as he stroked his hand across her pubic thatch, letting the tips of his fingers caress the lips of her already damp cunny. Her body began to vibrate as he found her clitty which he began to rub in a slow, insistent rhythm. 'O-o-o-h! O-o-o-h! O-o-o-h!' she breathed heavily as in turn she started to rub his throbbing tool in time with his teasing of her twitching little clitty.

He continued to frig her, deftly tucking his hand between her quivering thighs, feeling her pussy getting wetter and wetter as she fucked herself on the three fingers which he now slid in and out of her honeypot.

'God, my pussy's so juicy,' Julie cried softly. 'Slide your prick inside me, darling, and let's fuck the night away!'

She parted her legs as Ivor climbed over her and slid his shaft in her wet, willing cunny channel as she sighed with unalloyed delight. As their pubic hairs meshed together he tweaked one of her glorious red nipples with his tongue as she wriggled happily underneath him. He fucked her with long, hard strokes and the walls of her clinging cunny felt like moist, ribbed velvet around his cock. He changed the pace of his pistoning to one of short, sharp jabs and he cupped her bum cheeks as she rocked to a series of explosive climaxes, and the muscles of her love channel tightened around his shaft in a rippling seizure which ran from the tip of his prick down to the very root of his penis.

Again she contracted her juicy sheath and Ivor gasped as a second clutching spasm travelled the length of his prick. This sweet sensation made him powerless to resist his oncoming orgasm and the spunk burst out of his knob, forcing its way into her honeypot as gush after gush jetted through his twitching tool, spurting uncontrollably up her cunt, splashing its walls with frothy white foam.

Julie moaned and ground her pussy against his crotch as she achieved a final, stupendous climax. Her teeth sank into his shoulder as she arched her back, her breasts crushed against his heaving chest as their love juices leaked out to flood over their thighs, as slowly their passion subsided and Ivor reached down into her tangy wetness and smeared it over her succulent nipples whilst she copied his action by rubbing a blob of sticky cream from around his knob over his chest. A warm wave of fatigue washed over them and they lay there in silence on the crumpled sheets, at peace with themselves and the world, until Julie exclaimed with a start: 'I'd better have a look at my chicken, and I want to start cooking the rice. Don't go away now, I may well want to see you when I come back.'

She returned a few minutes later and sat down on the bed. She playfully took hold of Ivor's flaccid prick which was dangling over his thigh and pulled his foreskin up and down, capping and uncapping the smooth purple dome of his knob. 'All is well in the kitchen,' she announced cheerily as she noted his burgeoning erection with evident satisfaction, 'but I don't think the bird will be tender enough for another quarter of an hour.'

'Then come back to bed for a cuddle,' said Ivor lazily, and she obediently swung her legs up and made herself a nest for her head in the crook of his shoulder. 'Well, it's not as sunny in London as it is in Crete and we both have to work hard for our daily bread. Don't you miss the easy-going life out there?'

'Even lying in the sun doing very little can pall,' she replied with a sigh. 'Though at the beginning I loved the fun-filled late nights and sleeping till ten to wake up to a slow, sunshiny day, after a time I found myself wishing to be back in grimy old London.

'Truthfully, though, I suppose it all went sour when things started to go very wrong between Takis and myself,' she reflected thoughtfully. 'The relationship bloomed during the first months and almost every day was like a party. I think I liked the late afternoon best when we'd go down to the beach and we'd wait till the tourists had gone home.

'And then when no-one was around we would strip off our clothes and swim naked in the warm sea. Takis loved to lick me out afterwards. He would stand me up against a palm tree, spread my legs and kneel down in front of me. I'd hold his head in a firm grip and he would begin by licking my toes and ankles, trailing his warm, moist tongue up the insides of my legs until he reached my pussy.

'This invariably brought out the animal in me and I was always soaking wet and waiting impatiently to be frigged by his tongue and fingers. But Takis would always tease me first, flicking the tip of his tongue over and around my clitty before thrusting it in and eating me so sensuously whilst he frigged my cunny with his fingers, that I would come so quickly that I'd drench his face with my love juice. Whenever I did this he would get a massive erection and he'd wank himself off as he tongued me before we'd slide down upon the sand and we'd make love. Quite often, though, he would come too quickly as he'd been handling himself too vigorously whilst he was sending me off with his tongue. So it was usually best when he fucked me Greek style, if you know what I mean—'

'Via the tradesmen's entrance,' said Ivor helpfully, squeezing one of her deliciously firm, creamy buttocks.

Julie gave a low little chuckle and went on: 'That's one way of putting it. I'd never even heard of anal sex before and, to be honest, I didn't know he was going to try anything but make love doggie-style, when one night after we'd gone to bed, he flipped me over on to my tummy and parted my bum cheeks as he clambered up on to his knees behind me. Of course, I assumed that he was just going to take me from behind, but I turned round and saw Takis smearing his shaft with some greasy sun tan ointment. He gave me a wolfish grin and said: "I'm going to fuck your bottom, Julie – don't worry, I promise I won't hurt you."

'I wasn't too keen about the idea, but I'll try anything once and so as he instructed, I buried my face in the pillow and stuck out my bottom. He placed his knob between my buttocks and inserted the tip of his knob into my bum-hole. "Ouch!" I cried out as he pushed his prick forward. "Ow! That *does* hurt, Takis."

'But I relaxed as he drove forward a second time and he managed to push in about two inches of his prick, which caused me no problem, even when he began to fuck me. He started to ride in and out of my arse at will, passing his hands round to twiddle my elongated red nipples whilst he kissed the nape of my neck. Somehow, he managed to insert all his cock inside my bum – his tool was one of the longest I'd ever seen but it was not very thick, which I suppose must have helped matters as he corked me to the limit, gathering me at the waist to pull me back so that my bum cheeks were drawn up against his flat tummy. Then he sneaked a hand round to play with my pussy whilst I worked my bum from side to side, and this brought him off and he flooded my back passage with his sticky ejaculation.

'"Well, did you enjoy that?" he asked, his semi-stiff cock still embedded in my bottom. "Very nice," I replied, wriggling forward until his prick popped out of my bum-hole with a 'plop'. "Takis, I don't mind being fucked that way occasionally, but I really prefer to have my pussy seen to, if you don't mind."

'He didn't reply but looked rather disappointed and, from then on, our relationship began to flounder. Suddenly he had business to do which meant he had occasionally to stay overnight in Heraklion, but we really began to drift apart after we went to a club and during a wild after-hours party, two Swedish girls stripped themselves off and performed an erotic lesbian dance together in front of us. Takis became very excited watching them and then he shocked me by unzipping his trousers and exposing his naked stiff prick. "I'll do anything for you if you'll suck my cock," he whispered in my ear and, as we were sitting in a dark corner of the room so that with luck no-one would see me, I decided to please him, thinking that perhaps if I did as he asked, it would bring us close together again.

'So I slipped down under the table and took hold of his hard, quivering prick. I rubbed the pulsating pole, making it leap and bound in my right hand, as with the left I searched for his two soft balls, letting my nails scratch lightly across the hairy skin. Then I fed his prick unhurriedly into my mouth, letting the cherry helmet ease backwards and forwards over my tongue. I looked up to see if he was enjoying it and saw that his eyes were closed and he was groaning quietly with pleasure as I gently squeezed his balls. I continued by rolling my tongue up into a little wet arrow which circled his mushroomed knob, and then I slightly raised my head and powered my mouth down, sucking in his helmet, first just holding it and then exploring the pulsing shaft with the inside of my mouth and my now flattened tongue.

'Then I gave Takis's cock a slow, loving suck, working my tongue round the ridge of his knob, and his shaft throbbed even harder as I upped the pace, drawing the knob in and out between my lips faster and faster, lashing his rampant rod until he couldn't hold back any longer and he spurted great globs of sperm down my throat. He passed me a cloth napkin and I wiped his cock clean before getting up again and sitting down at the table as if nothing had happened.'

Julie looked across at Ivor and saw that her frank story had so excited her lover that his penis had swollen up and was standing up stiffly between his thighs. She let her fingers meander round the uncapped, swollen helmet of his pulsating prick, but then removed them as she said: 'No, we haven't time to make love right now. But it doesn't matter as we've the whole night ahead of us, haven't we? So do you want to put some clothes on, or if you like we could eat in the nude.'

'What a super idea! Doesn't it sound wicked!' enthused Ivor as he swung himself off the bed. 'I've never done that before and I'd love to try it. If we feel chilly we can always turn on the central heating.

'Just promise me, though, that you won't spill anything hot over my balls!' he added as he followed her out of the bedroom and into the dining room. He thoroughly enjoyed Julie's Chicken Paprika and the sight of her jiggling, naked breasts added an extra spice to the food.

Afterwards he help her to pile the plates into the dishwasher and they retired back to bed. 'What are you doing this weekend? Can we see each other tomorrow night?' asked Ivor, but he was disappointed to hear that Julie had promised her parents that she would go down and visit them in Frinton-on-Sea over the weekend. 'I'll have to stay through till Sunday afternoon as a couple of aged aunts are coming over to tea, though I should be back in London by about seven o'clock,' she added.

'Damn and blast it! Brian Lipman and I are taking the sleeper to Scotland on Sunday evening,' he said sadly.

'We're spending three days up there on this promotion for a new dog food. How about Thursday night, though? Pencil in dinner with me in your diary.'

'Call me when you get back to town, Ivor. It should be okay, but I am on the short-list for a four-day shoot in Malta with Mike Barklay.'

Ivor frowned and said: 'Mike Barklay, did you say? Would that be Mike Barklay, the famous glamour photographer?'

'Yes, he's choosing three girls for a big nudie spread in *Ram* and I'll know on Monday if I'm in line for the trip. He's also taking some pictures for a calendar to be put out by a big manufacturer of men's shirts.'

'Rather an odd choice, then, to use Mike Barklay and have pictures of girls without any shirts or anything else on,' grunted Ivor with a hint of irritation in his voice. 'Still, I suppose they hope to attract the punters.

'Anyway, good luck, darling, you should earn a nice few bob if you make the trip,' he said, trying to sound more enthusiastic than he felt about Julie baring all for Mike Barklay, a handsome young photographer from Liverpool whose pictures of The Beatles and other Merseyside pop groups had catapulted him into the columns of the popular newspapers.

Ivor had never actually met the photographer whose volume of nude studies had so shocked some of the bookselling fraternity that they had banned the book, which naturally ensured that it became a bestseller both in Britain and in the United States. Barklay had also nurtured a fearsome reputation as a Lothario and scarcely a month went by without his name being linked with a leggy model or film starlet in the gossip columns.

His disgruntlement was noticed by Julie, who giggled as she tickled him under the chin. 'My God, Ivor, you've only known me a little over twenty-four hours and already you're jealous! That's a bit strong, isn't it?'

He pondered over her question for a few moments and then finally answered with a chuckle: 'Yes, of course it is, and I apologise for being such a silly twit. It's really not my business whether you decide to take on nude work, even with such a notorious cocksman as Mike Barklay.'

'Good, for despite what's happened between us, I'm not in the habit of jumping into bed with every Tom, Dick or Ivor who comes to my rescue when my car breaks down!' she said, emphasising her words by tapping her finger across Ivor's lips, and he opened his mouth, trapping her finger between his teeth as he pulled her closer to him.

In a trice her finger was replaced by her soft lips and their tongues began to fly around in each other's mouths as she guided his hand to her breasts, and he flicked her nipples between his fingers until they stood up like two little red bullets. Then he trailed his hand downwards across her smooth belly to the silky dark bush, and slid his finger between the yielding cunny lips. Almost at once he found her clitty and started to massage the ribbed flesh as Julie whispered: 'Oh, Ivor, you're making me so randy! Now I want you to fuck me with your big, stiff cock. My pussy's wet enough already!'

Ivor wasted no time in placing himself above her and Julie parted her legs in grateful anticipation, drawing up her knees to give his cock easier access to her pouting love lips. He pressed himself against her, one hand squeezing her breast with his thumb wildly flicking against the rosy stem of her nipple, whilst the other hand slid down her spine and delved between the fleshy globes of her bottom. The tip of his forefinger was on the wrinkled little rosette of her arsehole which opened to his probing and, without demur, allowed the first joint of his finger to slide inside it. He used Julie's buttocks to lever her firmly upwards, bringing the entrance to her cunt in alignment with the uncapped, round knob of his searching prick.

The warm, moist grooves of her cunny fitted welcomingly around his tool and Julie pressed her hands down on his bum cheeks as, at the same time, she jerked her hips forward which made Ivor gasp as a gush of love juice flowed over his pulsating penis. He was now fully inside her and he lay quite still as he whispered: 'I'm fully in you, every inch of me . . . and now I'm going to fuck you, Julie.'

Julie looked up at him with a saucy glint in her eyes. 'Promises, promises! I want you to fuck the arse off me, Ivor!'

He growled his acceptance of this order and her thighs shook as Ivor embedded his full length inside her, feeling the folds of inner flesh pulse excitingly against his deeply buried shaft, and he dragged himself backwards before thrusting forwards and burying his cock to the hilt, grinding his groin roughly against hers before he pulled back again for another onslaught.

Julie writhed as her cunt contracted in hot, exciting spasms as Ivor's prick rammed forcefully in and out of her love channel. Again and again he plunged his throbbing tool into her squelchy wetness as he fucked her with long, sweeping strokes, slewing his cock in and out of her sopping pussy which sent delightful pulses of pleasure all along his shaft.

'Start spunking, I'm coming, I'm coming!' Julie screamed as she felt the oncoming orgasm building up quickly inside her, and she lifted her pelvis to meet him as he slammed his rock-hard shaft in and out of her cunt, faster and faster with his balls banging against her bum cheeks until his cock trembled and a huge fountain of sticky spunk tumbled into her cunny as they both shuddered with delight at the explosive force which racked their bodies as they climaxed together.

'Oh, you are so beautiful,' murmured Ivor as they lay quietly side by side in each other's arms. 'You will stay the night, won't you?'

'Yes, but I must be away early as I promised my parents I'd be home for lunch tomorrow,' Julie replied, but Ivor noticed that she had seemed lost in thought, mulling over something in her mind.

'Julie, is anything the matter?' he asked softly,

wrapping his arm around her shoulders. 'What's on your mind?'

She sat up and hugged him as she said: 'Sorry, I wasn't really miles away but I'm a bit worried, Ivor, about what's happening between us. Here we are, tumbling into a relationship far too quickly for my liking. We're already lovers after only a couple of days yet we hardly know anything about each other. And after Takis, I'm frightened of getting hurt again, I really am.'

'I can understand that, but we've not made any promises to each other, have we?' said Ivor, who whilst genuinely concerned to keep Julie's friendship, had no thoughts in mind except to continue the relationship on the present level.

'I've made no promises to you, nor have you to me. As far as I'm concerned, we're both free agents,' he emphasised and, in fairness, although he was a master at persuasion, Ivor never made rash promises in order to inveigle even the most desirable women into his bed. 'Are you saying you want to cool things and not see me on Thursday evening?' he added bluntly.

'No, I do want to see you on Thursday, honest I do. I'm just being silly, that's all,' said Julie, snuggling back onto his chest. 'But I know all about these promotion trips out of town. I bet you'll be in bed with some Scottish lassie on Monday night.'

Ivor chuckled and gave her a reassuring squeeze. 'Now who's getting jealous, then? Or are you just paying me back because I sounded grumpy when you told me that you might be working with Mike Barklay? Anyhow, I doubt very much if I'll even have the opportunity to screw around. But what you really want to know is if I'll be playing any Highland Games whilst I'm up in Scotland.'

'*Touché*, pussycat, and I'll bet you a pound that you'll get your leg over whilst you're away,' she retorted with spirit. 'Will you take the bet? I trust you to tell me the truth as to whether I've won or lost when we see each other on Thursday night.'

'Fair enough,' he agreed, pulling her hand down to caress his stiffening shaft as he kissed her on the lips. 'Now how about tossing my caber for a bit, h'mm?'

In fact, although they wrestled together for a few minutes, both were now too sleepy to begin a further bout of love-making and they soon fell fast asleep. Julie was first to wake the next morning and, after hastily slipping on her clothes, she scribbled a note for Ivor and was about to leave it on the bedside table when he opened his eyes and looked drowsily up at her. 'Bye bye, darling, I must be off, it's almost nine o'clock,' she said briskly, bending down to give him a quick kiss.

'Okay then, Julie, I'll call you from Glasgow,' he said drowsily. 'Have a nice weekend and give my regards to Frinton-on-Sea. Be a good girl and drive carefully now.'

'I will,' she promised and, kissing him again lightly on the cheek, made her way out of the bedroom and seconds later Ivor heard the front door close behind her.

❋ CHAPTER TWO ❋

An Exhausting Weekend

Ivor struggled out of bed an hour or so later when the postman rang the bell to deliver a recorded delivery letter. 'Hope it's a premium bond,' said the postman cheerfully, but Ivor groaned when he saw the address on the back of the buff envelope.

'No such luck, Fred, I copped two parking tickets from the same cow of a traffic warden last month and I'll bet this is a pay-up-or-else notice,' he sighed and the postman clucked his tongue in sympathy. 'Bad luck, Mr Belling. Some of those wardens are right sods, and I think the women are worse than the men. My brother's hopping mad about what happened to him a couple of weeks ago. He was leaving work after doing an early morning shift and was caught short in High Holborn, so he left his car outside the public loo whilst he went to have a slash, and when he came back there was a ticket slapped on his windscreen.

'Now how long does it take to relieve yourself? Two minutes, say? Three at the most, and even adding on thirty seconds for running up and down the stairs, the car couldn't have been parked there for five minutes. Yet when he came back there's a ticket saying he'd been there for seven minutes. Not right, is it?'

'No, it's not worth going to court, Fred, the magistrate won't believe you unless you've got the Archbishop of Canterbury and the Pope as witnesses. Anyhow, even three minutes is long enough for a warden to book you,' said Ivor, forbearing to ask why Fred's brother, who he knew also worked for the Post Office in nearby Bloomsbury Street, hadn't used his office loo but had rushed off to use a public convenience two minutes away which was a notorious meeting place for homosexuals.

He grunted a goodbye to Fred and, after dousing himself under a shower, he decided that he would tidy up the flat and have brunch at Louis's café in Hampstead before meeting Martin Reese and going on to Craven Cottage to see Fulham take on Chelsea, their mighty neighbours who were at present top of the league whilst already the home team were scrabbling about at the foot of the division, too near for comfort from the relegation places.

Ivor slipped the *Daily Mirror* under his arm and walked down to his garage and unlocked the door of his new Vauxhall Viva. Quite a comedown from driving a Bentley convertible, he thought, but the small car was comfortable and reliable – even though he had originally baulked at paying almost six hundred pounds for the de luxe model. The twenty-nine foot turning circle made for easy parking, which helped him manoeuvre his way into a small space in Heath Street opposite the famous continental patisserie where he found a table and ordered coffee and croissants before settling down to read his newspaper.

But only moments after he had sat down he was startled by a hand being clapped firmly on his shoulder, and he looked up to see a fair-haired young man of his own age beside him. 'Hello, Ivor, haven't seen you around on Saturday mornings for some time. Been on holiday, have you?'

Ivor folded his paper and flapped a hand in greeting. 'Hi Eugene. No, I took an early break in June but I've been out of town for the last three weekends. And what's new with you?'

'Nothing good, dear, I'm afraid,' replied Eugene glumly. 'Mind if I join you?' Ivor gestured for him to sit down and asked if he would like a coffee when the waitress brought his croissants to the table.

'Thanks, Ivor, I wóuldn't say no,' said his new companion, slumping down in the seat across the table. Eugene Lagner was the brother of a girl Ivor had dated some five years back and with whom he had kept friendly after they had broken up. He was an actor who made a reasonable living, mostly from small roles in television, although his name was usually to be found towards the end of the cast list. However, unlike so many in his profession, Eugene was rarely out of work as he was not untalented, and his slightly effeminate good looks were often also seen in minor movie roles. Furthermore, a year after leaving stage school, he had spent a summer as the willing live-in companion of a casting director who belonged to the gay brotherhood which existed in the top echelons of show business and looked after those in the close-knit fraternity.

'What's wrong, Eugene? I saw you on the telly in *Z*

Cars last week and aren't you in this new children's serial Granada TV is putting out next month?'

'My agent's supposed to be getting the contract next week, but I've got a terrible feeling that they might withdraw it after Tuesday morning,' said Eugene gloomily. 'Between ourselves, Ivor, I've been very stupid. A couple of weeks ago I came back to town after doing a couple of days down in Bournemouth on film work. Well, there I was at Waterloo Station so I decided to pop into the loo there.'

'You went cottaging, you mean,' said Ivor unsympathetically, as he had twice been accosted by homosexuals in public lavatories, although he realised that apart from friends' homes and a few well-known pubs or Lyons Corner Houses, it was difficult for homosexuals to meet others of their ilk, and there was always the ever-present danger of blackmail or even arrest.

Eugene nodded and said: 'Well, you usually find a nice class of bloke there, much nicer than Charing Cross for some reason. Anyway, there I was, minding my own business, when I saw this young chap looking up and down at me with a smile on his face. So I popped Percy back in my trousers and sauntered over to him with my trousers unzipped and said: "Hello there, handsome, what's a nice boy like you doing in a place like this?" Then the next thing I know, another chap comes up behind me and I'm being done for soliciting. My case comes up on Tuesday and my lawyer says I don't have a hope of beating the rap, so it'll be in the *News of the World* next Sunday even if the other papers don't pick it up.'

'Well, you haven't been done before, have you, so you're not looking at prison. It'll be a fine or, if you're lucky, a conditional discharge,' mused Ivor. 'But it's the publicity that's the killer, isn't it?

'I'm not sure how you can get round that one,' he added as the waitress placed two coffees in front of them. Then as he looked up Ivor saw a familiar portly figure in the queue at the front of the shop for the famous cakes, tarts and pastries. 'Wait a minute, Eugene, if anyone can help you, the chap over there can,' he said, pushing back his chair. 'His name's Harold Brown and he's a solicitor in Ruthe and Brendah's office, you know, the firm which represents a lot of show business people.'

Eugene's face brightened up and he said: 'I've heard of them. They arranged Estelle Woodway's divorce from that American actor, Mike what's -his-name, and I'm sure they were involved with getting work permits for a couple of friends of mine in New York.'

'I know Harold quite well, we've met at parties and at bridge at my boss's house. He's a very decent sort of bloke and I know he'll help if he can. Hold on, I'll see if he's got a couple of minutes to spare.'

Ivor left the table and walked over to where Harold Brown was waiting to be served. Eugene looked on anxiously as he saw the two men converse, but relaxed when after making his purchase, Harold Brown accompanied Ivor back to the table. 'Hello there, Mr Lagner, I saw you in Z Cars last week didn't I? Must be fun to work with such a professional team. Still, Ivor here tells me that you've had a spot of bother with the law. Would you care to tell me all about it?'

After Eugene had recounted the whole story, Harold Brown drummed his fingers on the table. 'Well, there's only one possible way out,' he said, lowering his voice. 'And this is strictly off the record, of course. Ask your doctor to write a sick note for you on Monday and get a postponement of the case. You'll have at least a week, if not two, and what you must do is to make an appointment to see the arresting officers. Don't write, just make a 'phone call and ask to meet them in a pub or café as soon as possible. Say nothing more over the 'phone and if they don't take the bait, well, that's it, you'll have to take your chances in court. But if they do make a meet you tell them quietly that you'll make it worthwhile for them to drop the case. Slide over a couple of brown envelopes with fifty quid inside each one and don't say another word. Just get up and walk away. Now either you'll get a letter saying that on consideration of the facts you won't be prosecuted on this occasion but warning you of your future behaviour, or you're back to square one with a hundred quid less in the bank. But that's the only possible escape hatch, I'm afraid, and there's always the remote chance that they'll do you for attempted bribery, but I doubt that very much. After all, what you did isn't criminal in most civilised countries. If we reformed the law so that consenting adults could do what they like in private, you wouldn't have to frequent these seedy places, would you?'

'Too true, I only wish more people felt the same way,' said Eugene warmly. 'And I'm truly grateful for the unofficial advice. I'll think it over but I'll probably take a chance – after all, what have I got to lose? Now I must be off, I'm meeting a friend at twelve up on the Heath. Very nice meeting you, Mr Brown, and thanks for the coffee, Ivor, see you around.'

As they watched him disappear out into the street, Ivor commented: 'You're quite right, Harold, what people do in bed is hardly a matter for the law.'

'No, it isn't and it's about time things were changed. Almost everyone agrees that the law's totally out of date, though it takes so long for any social reform to take place,' said the young solicitor firmly. 'Why, it's more than seventy years since that famous Victorian actress, Mrs Patrick Campbell, made that famous remark about not caring what people got up to together, so long as they did it behind closed curtains and didn't frighten the horses!'

Ivor chuckled and said lightly: 'Ah well, I'm sure the woofters will be able to breathe more freely if we continue shaping this permissive society some of the papers are frothing at the mouth about. Anyhow, I haven't seen you for a month or so, Harold. Are you playing any bridge these days?'

Harold Brown shifted his large body uncomfortably in

his chair and grunted. 'It's funny you should ask me that, because I had a strange experience after a game of bridge last Wednesday night.'

'*After* the game, did you say?'

'Yes, I played at Ronnie Dunn's. I don't think you've met him, have you? He runs a couple of antique shops in Islington and makes a fortune flogging old junk to American tourists. Anyhow, as I was leaving my flat to go to Ronnie's, I had a telephone call from Doris, a girl I went out with a few years back. We drifted apart and the last I heard she married some fellow in the rag trade last year. I said I was going out but she begged me to go round to her place whatever time I could. "My husband's coming home early tomorrow morning and I won't have a chance to speak to you unless we can meet later tonight. I never go to bed till one o'clock anyway, so you won't disturb me if you come round after your game."

'As it happens I had a rotten game. I lost about five quid, though we play for very small stakes. The cards just weren't with me. If I picked up a good hand, my partner had nothing and whenever I needed a finesse or a suit breaking well, it always went against me. Anyhow, towards the end of the evening I was feeling more than a bit disgruntled and wasn't sorry when one of the others wanted to pack up early as he had to go to Frankfurt early the next morning. So it was only a quarter to twelve when I rang Doris's door-bell. She came to the door herself, dressed in a diaphanous cream robe, and was obviously very pleased to see me. "Oh Harold, thank you for coming so quickly," she said, kissing me on the cheek as she ushered me in.

'She offered me a brandy, which I accepted, and I could see from the half-filled glass by her chair that she had already been sampling the bottle of Remy Martin. "Well, what's the trouble, Doris?" I said, coming straight to the point. "How can I help you?"

'"It's Steve, my husband. He's having an affair with his secretary," she said, but before I could ask the usual first question she raised a finger and went on: "No, there's no doubt about it, I have the evidence. Read this, Harold, and tell me if that isn't good enough proof for anyone."

'She took out a well-creased sheet of paper and passed it over to me. Here, I've got it with me. I shouldn't really show it to you, Ivor, but you don't know the parties involved and I know you won't breathe a word to anyone.'

He passed the paper over to Ivor who quickly scanned the typewritten letter which read:

Dearest Steve,

I can hardly wait till Wednesday night when you will once again be in my arms. Didn't we make love so magically last night? You must try to get away from home more often. Let me remind you of what you are missing. I'm sitting quite naked on my bed as I write and I'm still feeling very sexy, even though as you're not here I've had to finish myself off.

Shall I tell you how I did it? First I ran my hands all over my breasts and then I rolled my palms against the upright red titties as I pressed my breasts together and licked the erect rubbery nipples. This made me feel so randy that I closed my eyes and slowly slid my hand down between my legs where I could feel the juices already moistening my pussy. I inserted a finger and moved it around, thinking how much I really wanted your big, thick cock inside me instead. My thumb is a poor substitute for your lovely prick and I wish my fingers were elsewhere, preferably raking your back as your rampant rod pumps in and out of my eager crack.

Don't be late on Wednesday.
Love,
Jacqui

'Doris found this in her husband's raincoat pocket after he'd asked her to take it to the dry cleaners,' said the solicitor.

'Wow, it's hot stuff. What defence can her husband

have if this letter is produced in court?' said Ivor as he passed back the letter, but Harold wagged a warning finger. 'Oh, you'd be surprised,' he replied, tucking the letter back into his pocket. 'Only Jacqui's name is handwritten and either she or Steve could claim it's a forgery. Even if we could prove it was typed on a machine in the office, it wouldn't be conclusive, which is what I told Doris. I told her that girls do get crushes on their bosses and Steve could deny the whole business. After all, he would have to be pretty daft to forget he'd left a love letter in his raincoat when he asked his wife to take it to the cleaners.

'But the fact of the matter is that she wasn't that angry about Steve's infidelity. The marriage hadn't worked out, they had no children and this business gave her the excuse to leave him. "I should never have broken up with you, Harold," Doris said as she came across and sat on my lap. There was an awkward silence for a moment and then she kissed me and sucked my tongue into her mouth.

'Well, this was crazy, but as they say, a stiff prick has no conscience and I responded by slipping off her robe, and found that she was only wearing a transparent short nightie underneath it. I remembered what turned her on and began kissing her between her breasts, and she began to moan in the way which I knew signalled arousal. I slipped the straps of her nightdress from her shoulders and slid the garment off her firm breasts. She has the most sensitive nipples of any girl I've ever known, and when I took her tittie in my mouth her mouth fell open and she began to gasp and squirm. I ran my hands under her nightie and cupped her hairy mound, stroking her clitty whilst she tore open the zip of my flies and, once she'd brought out my cock, she planted a smacking wet kiss on my knob and juiced my shaft with saliva before sucking it in between her lips in huge, quick gulps.

'In a minute or so we were both naked and rolling around on the carpet. Doris had remembered how I had always loved to take her from behind, so she clambered up on all fours, sticking out her solid, well-rounded backside and spread her thighs wide to show off her juicy crack, bringing round her hand to spread her cunny lips wide open, frigging herself whilst she waited for my cock.

'My heart was racing wildly as I knelt behind her and slid my shaft between her bum cheeks and into her cunt. She gave a loud sigh of relief and moved her hips backwards towards me so that my cock was fully embedded inside her. Doris's love channel was as smooth and tight as ever and she had lost none of her marvellous knack of making her cunny muscles grip the entire length of my prick, letting me pause for a few moments to savour the wonderful sensations.

'Then, as I clasped hold of her breasts and squeezed the hard red nipples, she turned her pretty head round and panted: "Oooh, that's yummy, Harold, just like the old days. No, even better! Now fuck me properly – you don't have to worry, I'm on the pill."

'So I pushed in and out as fiercely as I could, burying my cock in her little love box and bending forward to hold those globe-like breasts, tweaking her titties as, just like in the old days when we were going out together, her arse responded to my shoves. I was so excited that I soon felt my balls tighten, and before I knew what was happening, I'd shot my load inside her dripping pussy.

'It really wasn't a very professional way to behave,' he added, stroking his chin as he thought back over the incident.

'You mean you should have held on till she managed to come?' said Ivor innocently.

'No, no, no, I don't mean that at all – what I was referring to was the fact that I'm a solicitor and we don't make a habit of bonking people who come to us for advice!'

'Well, Doris isn't your client, is she? You aren't going to send her in a bill, are you? Anyhow, what happened next? Did you make your excuses and make a hurried exit?'

Harold Brown took a deep breath and slowly exhaled it before replying. 'I should have done,' he admitted ruefully. 'But Doris then attacked my cock with her tongue and I would challenge any man to walk away from one of her blow jobs. She lay me down flat on my back and flicked her tongue along the underside of my knob. Doris only had to do this for about half a minute and my prick was as stiff as a poker again. Christ, how she gobbled away, sucking and slurping, plunging it in to wash it all over with her tongue and then pulling it in and out, faster and faster, till I was ready to come again.

'She sensed she had better stop or I would come again, so she rose up on her knees and straddled me, fitting my cock to her cunt, and started to slide up and down on my throbbing tool. I jerked upwards in time with her rhythm whilst helping Doris enjoy the ride even more by lifting my body up to suck on her titties, and this time she came before I spunked into her. Afterwards, as we lay panting on the carpet, Doris complimented me on my sexual prowess. "Harold, you always were my favourite fuck. A man who was always up to the mark, well hung and always trying to please his partner," she cooed sleepily as we lay on the carpet with my clothes bundled up as a makeshift pillow.'

'It sounds as if you were well compensated for having such a rotten game of bridge,' grinned Ivor, but Harold Brown did not return his smile when he replied: 'I was feeling fine up until then, but just after she spoke we heard the crunch of tyres on the gravel drive outside.'

'"Oh My God! It's Steve," she cried out wildly as she grabbed her robe and scrambled to her feet. "Quick, Harold, run upstairs and hide in one of the spare bedrooms. I'll leave your clothes behind the sofa so you can collect them when you come down again after Steve's gone to sleep."

'So I rushed upstairs, bollock naked, and ran through into the first room which caught my eye. I closed the door behind me and switched on the light and guess what – I'd only run into Doris and Steve's bedroom! I'll tip-toe across the landing into another room, I thought, but then the front door closed and I heard Steve call out: "Hello, darling, the meeting finished earlier than expected, so rather than stay overnight in Coventry I decided to pound down the motorway and come home instead. You're up very late, aren't you? It's well after midnight."

'"Yes, I couldn't sleep, but I will now that you're back – let's go up to bed straight away," urged Doris, no doubt wanting to shepherd her husband away from the lounge where my glass and the open bottle of brandy might cause some searching questions to be asked. I might have still had time to shoot out onto the landing and slip into another room, but I was paralysed with fear. By the time I decided to move, it was too late, for Doris and Steve were now climbing up the stairs. I looked round frantically for somewhere to hide and then I saw that her wardrobe was open. I dived inside, leaving the door slightly ajar so that I would be able to see when the coast was clear.

'Steve sat down on the bed and started to undress whilst Doris went into the bathroom to brush her teeth. He hung up his clothes and followed her into the bathroom. I heard the sounds of giggling and wondered again whether I should make a dash for the door, but before I could move, they came back together into the bedroom and I saw Steve caress his wife's breasts as he gave her a big kiss. To my horror she giggled: "Hold on a minute, let me undress first," as she freed herself from his embrace and walked across to the wardrobe.'

He paused dramatically and, as he mopped his brow, Ivor looked round and suddenly noticed with amusement that the babble of conversation at the two adjoining tables had ceased and that other customers were also straining to hear the end of Harold Brown's vivid tale.

'It must have been a toss-up as to who was scared most, you or Doris,' murmured Ivor sympathetically, and his plump companion nodded his agreement.

'You can say that again,' he continued warmly. 'Well, I

suppose I must give Doris full marks for coolness, for though she gave a little jump when she saw me squeezed in amongst her dresses, she said nothing but took off her robe and hung it up on a hanger. "Switch the light off, Steve," she called out as she half closed the door, but although her husband must have been exhausted from his long day at work and drive down the M1, he began to fondle his wife's creamy curves.

'"Aren't you too tired to fuck?" asked Doris as she slid her hand up and down his thick, swelling shaft. "I'm never too tired for that!" he grunted and, with his prick waggling in anticipation, he climbed on top of her. Doris opened her legs wide and I saw his meaty prick slide sweetly inside her juicy cunny and, thankfully, he was unaware that it had only recently been moistened by my John Thomas!

'"Now, Steve, give me a good seeing to!" yelled Doris wildly. "Pump that big prick of yours in out of my cunt! Oooh, listen to it squelching in and out between my love lips!" I could see his buttocks rise and fall until with a great shudder he spunked into her cunny as she squealed with pleasure. Then he withdrew his glistening shaft which still looked heavy and almost fully erect, and Doris made him life on his back and smoothed her hands over his chest. "M'mm, I think you've still got some spunk left in your balls, haven't you? Lie back and relax, darling, and I'll suck you off."

'He did as he was told and she ran her tongue up and down the length of his prick, which made it shoot up to its previous rock-hard fullness. "Aaaah, that's wonderful," he breathed and as she smacked her lips and sucked lustily away on her husband's throbbing tool, she beckoned me with her hand to come out of hiding. So I quietly opened the door and on tip-toe I crept out of the room as Doris gave me a cheery wave goodbye as she sucked lustily away on Steve's cock, moving her head up and down his thick shaft. I found my clothes behind the sofa, quietly dressed myself and let myself out of the front door. Luckily I had parked outside in the road, for I don't know how Doris would have bluffed it out if I had left it in the drive and Steve had seen my car when he came home.'

'My word, you were fortunate to get away scot-free,' said Ivor, calling for the bill from the waitress who was hovering nearby.

Harold Brown grunted and went on: 'Not exactly. You can imagine that I was in a hell of a hurry to get away, and I shot away as fast as I could. Well, the next thing I know is that I can see the headlights of a car behind me with a blue flashing light on its roof. To cut a long story short, I was booked for speeding, though I managed to talk my way out by going down to the station for a breath test and, thank God, the brandy I'd had at Doris's was the only drink I'd had all evening, except for a sherry before the bridge game, and the coppers could see that I wasn't under the influence.'

'So, it'll cost you a few quid. It isn't the end of the world,' Ivor commented, passing a ten shilling note to the waitress and waving away the proferred change.

'I suppose it could have been worse,' Harold Brown admitted, 'but the magistrates won't take kindly to a chap doing seventy-five down Finchley Road at two-thirty in the morning, especially as it'll be the third time I've been done for speeding during the last year. I was only going about forty-five when I was caught in a speed trap in Regents Park, and about the same speed when I was going home late one evening along Baker Street.

'Now here's the final twist, Ivor. I telephoned Doris a couple of days later and you'll never guess what she told me. She said that she'd been thinking it over and she'd decided to give Steve another chance, especially as he'd happened to mention the very next morning that Jacqui, the secretary who was supposed to have written that sexy letter I showed you, had given her notice in and would be leaving at the end of the week.'

'What a coincidence,' Ivor remarked. 'Do you believe her?'

The solicitor shrugged his shoulders. 'Maybe yes, maybe no, but I'm almost positive that Doris composed that letter herself. She was bored and needed to justify having a quick fling. Some people are like that, you know. They weave fact and fiction together and they begin to believe their own fantasies. Perhaps the experience will put some p'zazz back into her love life, but for sure, it's a fool who comes between a man and wife. I've always maintained it is very stupid to screw around with a married woman, and I should have taken my own good advice which I'm dishing out every week to the showbiz people who come into the office asking for help in sorting out their marital tangles.'

'Well, I've always held the same maxim and never fooled around with married women, it always ends up with tears,' Ivor declared as he stood up. 'I must be going, Harold. Martin and I are going to a football match this afternoon and I have to pick him up in ten minutes.'

'You a Fulham fan like Martin? Yes? You're real masochists, the pair of you. Why don't you go and watch a real team like Spurs?'

'Why did you diddle Doris?' Ivor retorted. 'We've all got a crazy streak somewhere in our make-up.'

'Yes, that's true enough,' sighed Harold Brown. 'I think I'll stay and drown my sorrows with a coffee and another slice of chocolate cake. Give Martin my regards and tell him I'm sorry about Fulham.'

Ivor chuckled and said: 'Hey, they haven't lost yet. Chelsea might be off form or have a couple of players out with injuries.'

'They would have to play without a goalkeeper for Fulham to win. Mind, we have the game down for a draw on the office pools coupon, so I really hope that you somehow manage to snatch a point.'

Ivor relayed this hope on to Martin Reese when he met his boss who was already standing outside on the pavement waiting for him. 'Harold knows fuck all about football,' Martin snorted angrily. 'I've half a mind to put a fixed odds bet on Fulham to win with another couple of games at the betting shop over there.'

Luckily, Ivor dissuaded the chairman of Cable Publicity, saying that he wanted to get to Craven Cottage early in order to park reasonably near the ground, and although Fulham failed to win, they helped Harold Brown's pools coupon by gaining a surprise one-all draw, because after taking an early lead, Chelsea wasted several simple opportunities to wrap up the game, and in the very last minute a careless back pass by a Chelsea defender to his defender let in Fulham's captain, Johnny Haynes, to tap the ball over the line for a valuable point.

'Well, with a bit more luck like that, we might stay up this season,' commented Ivor as he and Martin marched back towards the car.

'I certainly hope so,' said Martin. 'All they need is a couple of new players and they'd shoot up the table. Anyhow, what are you doing tonight? Which sexy, mini-skirted dollybird will you be screwing? Hell, I wish we could change places and I'll look after your date whilst you trundle off to Covent Garden.'

'I've nothing on for tonight,' Ivor replied as they came to a halt by his car and he unlocked the driver's door. 'And I'd genuinely love to hear Marchiano sing in *Turandot*. Do you remember the plot I sketched out for you in the office?'

'Just about, but I'll mug up on the programme before the curtain goes up,' said his boss as he climbed into the car. 'Switch on the radio and we'll hear the results on *Sports Report*.'

Later that evening Ivor sat in his flat, moodily contemplating a night spent falling asleep in front of the television. He had watched the Rolf Harris show if only to see the sexy Young Generation dancers, and he reflected on how strange it was that a hurried flash of a girl's knickers as she whirled around in a frantic dance routine was often more exciting than seeing the same girl in a far more revealing swimsuit on the beach.

'I can't bloody sit here all night,' he said aloud to the television set, stretching his arms as he yawned. 'I bet Julie's having a whale of a time . . . well, perhaps she isn't stuck down there with her folks in Frinton, but as she said, we made no commitment to each other. Sod it, I'm going out for a drink.'

His favoured bar was La Herradura, a small club near Finchley Road station where the foreign au pair girls gathered on Saturday and Sunday nights. The club owner, José, was a small, bearded Spaniard whose policy of allowing in only a reasonable number of men at any one time was much appreciated by Ivor and those few young Englishmen who successfully applied for club membership.

He greeted José at the entrance after he saw him turn away a group of some half dozen teenage boys from the door. '*Buenas tardes*, José,' said Ivor, jerking his thumb towards the departing crestfallen youths. 'Surely the club isn't full already, it's only a quarter past nine.'

'No, though we're pretty busy already,' growled José gruffly. 'I sent those kids packing because they looked too young for me. The girls who come here want to dance with men, not boys.'

'Hope you're right,' said Ivor, digging out his membership card, but José waved him through without even looking at it. He looked approvingly at the gaggle of girls sitting around and as usual was fascinated by the babble of different languages from the various tables. This was the only problem about trying to pick up girls at La Herradura, for quite a number of the girls spoke such poor English that it was impossible to make conversation after asking what they would like to drink. Like all the Englishmen who frequented the club, Ivor always searched around for the blonde Scandinavian girls who almost invariably spoke English, though he had also discovered that Swedish au pairs had an undeserved reputation for jumping into bed at the drop of a hat.

In the dim, smoky light he made his way to the bar and

ordered a Campari and soda. He tasted his drink, added a little more soda and then swung round to face the small dance floor where two girls were jiving together to the strains of one of Ruff Trayde's most popular numbers. Then he turned sharply as he felt a hand tug at his sleeve. To his pleasant surprise, he saw that the hand belonged to a ravishing girl dressed in a tight black dress who said to him in delightfully accented English: 'Oh, I am so sorry, I did not mean to startle you. But are you not Monsieur Ivor Belling?'

Fame at last, thought Ivor, as he smiled and said easily: 'Yes, I am, how did you know my name?'

She cocked her head slightly to the side and took a small step backwards. 'You don't remember me? I am the flatmate of your secretary Suzie Wilkinson and my name is Tanya Chirasonne. We met about two weeks ago when you brought Suzie home one evening after a reception and you came in for coffee.'

Christ, how could he have not recognised this stunning creature? 'Of course I remember you, Tanya. I didn't recognise you at first, that's all. You're staying with Suzie for six months while you take an intensive course in English, right? The funny thing is that Suzie's gone to France this weekend with her boy friend.'

'Yes, she's very lucky,' said Tanya, brushing back her tousled mane of silky dark hair. 'I would also have loved to spend the weekend in Paris, but how do you say, some people have all the luck.'

'May I buy you a drink?' offered Ivor, and to his delight she accepted and asked for a Scotch on the rocks. He caught the eye of the barman and ordered a double whisky, placing two big ice cubes inside the glass when the barman brought the drink over to him. He slid the necessary coins over the counter and they found two free seats at a table by the window.

'So what brings you to La Herradura, Tanya? It's quite a journey to Finchley Road from South Kensington and I would have thought there were plenty of bars and clubs near to where you live. You are still sharing with Suzie in Exhibition Road, aren't you?'

'Oh yes, I like living with Suzie very much. She is a sweet, kind girl and we get on very well together,' said Tanya, clinking her glass against Ivor's. '*Salut*, Monsieur Belling.'

'Cheers, but please let's not be formal – my name is Ivor,' he said, trying his best not to stare at Tanya's sloe eyes, dark and luminous in the high-cheekboned oval of her face. He cleared his throat and repeated: 'So what made you come all the way from South Kensington? Did you hear about this place from a friend?'

'Yes, Helene, one of my school friends is working as an au pair in Golders Green and she said we would meet interesting people from all over Europe at La Herradura, so we arranged to meet here.'

Ivor peered across the crowded room. 'Where is Helene? Perhaps she would like to join us for a drink.'

'That would not be possible, she left five minutes ago with her boy friend. He is taking her out to the country for a drive in his new car and though they asked me if I wanted to go with them, I said no, because what is the expression, now—'

'Two's company, three's a crowd,' supplied Ivor, and Tanya nodded her agreement. '*Oui, c'est ça*. And I would be, how do you put it, playing gooseberry, no?'

'Yes, very well said,' Ivor noted approvingly. 'I can see that you've managed to learn some useful colloquial phrases,' but when she looked blankly at him he added quickly: '*les expressions familière*.'

Tanya smiled broadly and briefly ducked her head in acknowledgment of his compliment. 'Thank you for saying so, though I still have much to learn. Still, my English is improving. There is nothing better than living in a country if you really want to learn the language.'

'Absolutely, I only learned to speak French properly after spending a summer in St Tropez, even though I passed all my school examinations,' said Ivor, who refrained from adding that what gave him the most pleasure during his stay in St Tropez was not gaining fluency in French, but finally losing his unwanted virginity during that glorious summer. 'I worked in a small hotel right in the centre of the resort for seven weeks and had a wonderful time, though if I ever stay there again, I'd prefer to go back as a guest!'

'Did you ever see Brigitte Bardot sunning herself on the beach?' asked Tanya with a twinkle in her eye.

'No, worse luck, there were lots of other gorgeous girls around,' he replied and launched himself into a panegyric of praise for French girls. 'You know something, Tanya, I'm not saying there aren't many lovely English girls because there are – for example, look at Suzie, isn't she beautiful? Yet anyone can see that French women have so much more style. They always look so chic and sexy, whilst I sometimes think that pretty English girls do everything they can to make themselves look ugly or masculine. They wear enormous hats to cover their faces or shapeless dresses if they have nice figures, and I have never understood why so many English girls don't bother to make themselves look more desirable.'

'Perhaps this is because Englishmen don't look at women the same way that Frenchmen do,' Tanya said thoughtfully. 'My uncle lived in London for many years and he says that English society puts up too many barriers between men and women, like the fact that boys and girls are taught in separate schools, and the old-fashioned gentlemen's clubs and women's institutes. But I think things are changing, are they not, here in Swinging London?'

'Let's hope so, Tanya,' said Ivor as he downed the dregs of his Campari and rose to his feet. 'Would you like another drink?'

'Later perhaps, but I'd rather dance a little first,' she said, looking up at him with a sensual smile. 'Great, so would I,' said Ivor and escorted her onto the tiny dance floor. They jived to frenetic rock n' roll but then the tape was changed to slow, bluesy music and Ivor thrilled to the feel of her soft, warm body pressed against him as they gently rocked from side to side, hemmed in by other couples who huddled up alongside them. His arms were wrapped around her shoulders whilst her hands were locked around the back of his neck, and he gasped when she lifted her face and gently kissed him on the lips. He had tried to control the stirrings in his groin, but now his penis swelled up and the rock-hard shaft insinuated itself against Tanya's tummy.

He attempted to draw his body back but the French girl opened her dark, almond-shaped eyes and without a word pulled him close to her again. When the record finished Ivor asked her again if she would like another drink, and this time she nodded, but said: 'Thank you, I'd like a coffee, please. I'll come with you, though, as I would like something to eat from the bar as I didn't have time to make supper because I had to take the underground train and a bus to meet my friend. Please let me buy you something whilst you get the drinks.'

Ivor shook his head. 'I'm afraid they don't serve any food here. Anyhow, I've a far better idea. I haven't had any supper tonight, either, so why don't we go to Chez Alain, one of my favourite restaurants. It's a little French bistro down the road less than five minutes walk away. They don't take bookings so we'll get a table eventually, but we can always have a drink in the bar whilst we wait. You'll love it, Tanya. The *bifteck et pommes frites* will make you think you're back home!'

'It sounds very nice but I will come only if we "go Dutch", that is the right English *expression familière, n'est pas?* Yes, I must pay my share of the bill,' she said firmly.

'Why on earth should I let you do that?' Ivor protested vehemently. 'It's my pleasure to take you there and well, frankly, I'm not short of money. Anyway, it isn't even an expensive restaurant.'

'But it was my suggestion that we have something to eat,' she pouted and would have continued if Ivor had not placed a restraining finger on her lips. 'Please don't argue with me,' he begged, looking straight into her deliciously dark liquid eyes. 'The next thing will be you offering to pay for the petrol when I drive you home!'

Tanya laughed and squeezed his arm. 'Well, Suzie told me that you were a generous man, but I wouldn't want you to think that I was taking advantage of you,' she commented as she picked up her handbag and they made their way out to the cloakroom.

Usually there was a patient queue at Chez Alain, but a table for two fell vacant only a few minutes after Ivor and Tanya arrived. They chatted animatedly over their meal and the *bifteck et pommes frites* was as tasty as Ivor had promised, and made even more delicious by being eaten with a bottle of the restaurant's best Beaujolais which Ivor had ordered as soon as they had sat down at their table.

Tanya refused the offer of a dessert, saying that she had to watch her weight, but she might nibble a piece of his *tarte aux pommes*. 'This has been a marvellous if unexpected treat,' she said as she watched Ivor tuck into a sizeable portion of apple tart.

'I could say exactly the same thing,' said Ivor, crunching his teeth through the soft pastry. 'Now, how about some coffee?'

'Well, as you won't let me contribute to the bill, at least let me make you coffee at the flat,' declared Tanya, a suggestion which Ivor was more than happy to fall in with and he grinned. 'I won't disagree with you there, let me just get the bill.'

They walked arm in arm out of the restaurant and Ivor guided her across the road to his car, and twenty-five minutes later he was parking the Viva outside the door of the flat Tanya shared with Suzie, Ivor's secretary. He followed Tanya inside and after they had thrown their coats over a chair, Tanya told him to go straight through the narrow hall into the lounge.

'I'll be with you in a moment,' she called out and Ivor

110

assumed that she was going into the kitchen to put on the kettle. After a few moments he went to the door and, peering round it, he noticed through the wide open door that the kitchen was in complete darkness.

'Tanya?' he called out questioningly, and then he noticed that another door leading off the hallway was slightly ajar, which he assumed was either Suzie's or Tanya's bedroom. He slowly pushed it open and then he caught his breath sharply as in the soft light from a bedside lamp he saw Tanya standing by the bed. She was extraordinarily lovely with her eyes dark and moist and her hair falling loosely over her bare shoulders as she tugged down the zip on the side of her dress. The black garment fell down to her feet and she stepped out of it with graceful ease, her glistening body shining like satin, reflecting the light. Tanya was now naked except for a half cup bra over which her generous breasts spilled so excitingly, and matching lacy panties that were pulled up tightly over her mound, exposing the outlines of her love lips.

She smiled at him and said throatily: 'Shut the door behind you, Ivor, I was coming inside to you but as you're here you have saved me the journey.'

Ivor gulped and held himself in check for he could scarcely believe that this beautiful, sexy girl was offering herself to him. She moved forward and unhooked the bra, throwing it to the ground. Her jutting breasts swung like pendulums as she approached him, and for a moment they stood facing each other without speaking as he passed his hands along the silky curves of her thrilling young body.

She looked at him invitingly and offered him her lips. He kissed her tenderly as they slid into a tightly held warm embrace and then, drawing breath, he kissed her again with a fiery urgency, his hands roaming over her breasts as the two of them fell back onto the bed.

'Take off your clothes,' she murmured and she helped him tear off his shirt and trousers and, when he was naked, Ivor felt Tanya's fingers moving deftly across his body, sliding along his belly, arousing every inch of flesh as she played with his pubic hair, moving around the base of his throbbing penis. His mouth opened wordlessly in suspense as now her fingertip ran through a tiny rivulet between the hairs and slid along the underside of his shaft, tracing a pattern around his tightening ballsack. Finally her hand closed around his pulsating prick and her long fingers sensuously worked their way up and down his tool, slowly frigging his cock up to an even greater stiffness.

Then she leaned across him to take the ruby-coloured knob in her mouth, her wet lips straining to encircle the smooth purple dome. She sucked some three inches of the shaft into her soft mouth and slid her head up and down until she had taken it all deep into her throat. Ivor placed his hands on her legs and pulled them over his body so that her pert young backside was directly over his mouth. He rolled down her panties to expose her rounded bum cheeks and, still with her lips clamped firmly around his gleaming cock, Tanya raised her feet so that Ivor could fling the panties away and allowed the beautiful French girl to lower her naked bottom lasciviously upon his face.

Ivor parted her buttocks and feasted his eyes on the delicate dribble of honey which was dripping from her cunt. He plunged his tongue through, licking, flicking and sucking as he flung his arm round Tanya's face and their two bodies dissolved into one as they lapped lustily away in a classic *soixante neuf*.

But Tanya rightly sensed that if she continued gorging on Ivor's quivering cock, he would very soon shoot his spunk inside her mouth. So she lifted her head and twisted round to lie on her back, her legs open as she ran a finger delicately along her slit and murmured: 'Now you must make love to me, Ivor, my pussy is aching to be fucked by your big cock.'

'I bet you didn't learn those words from your language school!' he said, and the idea of a gaggle of foreign girls sitting demurely at their desks whilst their English teacher

112

pointed to the words 'Fuck', 'Cock' and 'Cunt' on the blackboard for some reason tickled his funnybone, and he chuckled wildly. Tanya joined in and they shook with laughter until the convulsion died away and, for a moment, they looked at each other in silence.

Then he climbed over her and their lips flattened together and their tongues darted into each other's mouths whilst Ivor rubbed his bursting cock against her rubbery cunny lips, which at once slid open and he buried his shaft to the hilt inside her sweet honeypot.

At first he struck up a slow, regular rhythm and as his penis slid in and out of her juicy cunt, his hands worked in unison over her engorged strawberry nipples. They moved together with an easy grace, each sending thrills through the other time and again. Ivor moved his hands to Tanya's smooth, rounded bottom, massaging her soft buttocks with every stroke of his cock as steadily he increased the tempo of the coupling and their bodies thrust together, their hearts and minds concentrated totally on the joint intensity of their passionate love-making.

Ivor's penis began to twitch uncontrollably and Tanya realised that his climax would soon be upon him as the first long-drawn-out shudder of her own orgasm started to sweep over her. She reached down and cradled his balls which in seconds caused him to flood her love channel with his hot, creamy jism. As she felt the first surge of sperm splash against the walls of her cunny she trembled all over as an electric glow of satisfaction warmed her body.

'More! More! More!' Tanya cried out, desperate to prolong this frenzied fire of fulfilment, gripping him with her thighs and forcing him even deeper inside her as she milked his cock of every last drain of spunk in one final contraction until he slumped down on top of her. She felt his prick deflate inside her sopping cunny and so she pushed him over on to his back and bent forward to lick the last, prized drops of semen from the tip of his shrivelling shaft, before his knob disappeared like a rabbit bolting into its hole as his foreskin covered the purple crown. She ran her hands over his wrinkled ballsack and then rubbed her fingers around in the stickiness of his crinkly pubic bush. Ivor was at first puzzled by her action until she held his wrists tightly and drew them down to her own wet, hairy patch. Then he rubbed and fondled her pussy until she raised his fingers to her lips and licked him clean. He repaid the compliment, sucking and swallowing the jism from her fingers, and then they settled down for a much-needed post-coital sleep.

A blissful smile spread over Ivor's face as he slowly crossed the fuzzy border into semi-consciousness, for he had been dreaming that a beautiful girl was licking and lapping at his stiff, throbbing penis. His eyes fluttered open and to his delighted astonishment he discovered that the delicious sensation in his groin was no dream but actual reality! Tanya's hair was sprawled over his thighs as, with both hands clasped around the base of his erect cock, his lusty partner's lips were slurping around the uncapped crown of his erect prick.

He growled softly as he thrust his slippery shaft deeper into her mouth as she slid her lips over his knob and drew her warm, wet tongue down his rampant rod whilst she played with his hairy balls. He clutched at her hair and shivered as she circled the tip of her tongue all around the smooth flesh of his helmet, paying particular attention to the sensitive ridge.

Then Tanya performed her party piece. Removing her hands from Ivor's twitching tadger and clasping them together behind her back, she sucked up almost his entire thick shaft between her lips, bobbing her head up and down as she slurped avidly on the veiny pole which, true to form, jerked wildly in her mouth before shooting a jet of frothy jism down her throat. She greedily swallowed his spunk in four or five gulps, pulling him hard into her mouth until the last drops had been ejaculated and his prick started to shrink back to its normal size.

'*Formidable*,' sighed Ivor, running his hands through her hair as she now lay still with her head resting on his thighs. 'I don't think a girl can learn how to suck a cock so wonderfully. It is a natural talent.'

'Thank you, Ivor, you are not the first man to say this to me, but unfortunately, my cocksucking led to a disagreement with my previous boyfriend and we don't see each other any more,' Tanya said sadly.

'Good God! The man needs his head examined,' exclaimed Ivor, and seeing from the blank expression on her face that this was a colloquialism which had passed Tanya by, he added: 'I mean to say that your old boyfriend is crazy, *très stupide*. What more could he have asked for?'

She shrugged her shoulders as she brought her hands round to idly play with his shrunken shaft. 'Well, I will tell you. My boyfriend's name is Mark Osbourne and he lives very near here in one of those new luxury flats at Prince's Gate. We first met in June when I was sitting on a bench in Hyde Park and Mark's big Labrador dog came over and began jumping up and licking my face like I was a long lost friend. I still have a suspicion that Mark trained the dog to do this only on his command, though he always denied it.

'Anyhow, he apologised on behalf of his dog and then we began talking and, after a while, he asked if he could see me again. It was a whirlwind romance – within a hectic week he took me dancing, to the theatre and the ballet and one day he took me to Ascot Races in the Royal Enclosure and, although I objected, he insisted on buying me a new outfit for the occasion at an expensive shop in Bond Street. "Don't worry about it, Tanya," he said, pulling me into the shop after I had hesitated about going in. "My partner and I own this place as well as two other shops in Oxford Street, plus four more in Manchester, Nottingham, Leeds and Edinburgh."'

'Mark must be a very wealthy guy,' commented Ivor as he stroked his fingers tenderly through her hair and she purred contentedly as she said: 'Oh, that's nice, I do like that – and it costs nothing except your time, which was a lesson I was always trying to teach Mark who thought that he could simply buy my affection.'

'You mean he expected you always to say yes to anything he wanted,' said Ivor, and Tanya gave a tiny laugh. 'No, to be fair to Mark, he often asked me what I wanted to do when we were going out. For example, I could decide which film we should see or whether I preferred to go dancing or out to the country for a drive in his MG sports car.

'But then one evening he told me that he knew about some amazing sex parties which were being held every week here in Kensington. "Some very famous people are involved," he said to me as we lay in bed after we had made love and I had sucked him off. "Pop groups, some pretty actresses, two well-known Tory politicians, film stars and, I'm told, even a member or two of the Royal Family! I've never been to an orgy, have you? I wonder what it would be like."

'I was shocked to hear him speak like this and I told Mark very firmly that I was not at all interested in taking part in such a business, but then he said: "No, I suppose it would not be very nice to fuck in front of complete strangers. But how about us having a very select little party here in bed, just you and me with a couple of chaps like my best friends Andrew Edwards and Charles Windsor. Now that could be great fun, couldn't it?"

'"No, I don't think so," I said, but without so much conviction as the idea of making love with two men at the same time was a fantasy which I had sometimes thought about, and Mark must have suspected this because he began to tease me, saying: "Oh, come on, Tanya, you'd love to have me fuck you from behind whilst you're on your knees sucking Andrew's huge cock – and believe me, it really is huge, I promise you. Andrew and I were at boarding school together and he won the dormitory Thick Prick contest every year. You would so enjoy gobbling it, I know you would. Again I told Mark that I was not interested but, frankly, the idea did make me tingle all over as I thought a little more about it.

'Anyhow, Mark said no more until the next night after we had got back to his flat after spending the evening at a gambling club in Mayfair. Perhaps I should have realised what he had in mind when Andrew and Charles greeted us at the club. But I was in a good mood as Mark had given me ten pounds to play with at roulette and, though I lost at first, with my last chip I backed number nineteen – that's how old I am – and the number came up! So I paid Mark back, but I had still won twenty-five pounds. Mark had also won a few pounds so we were both in a very good mood when we arrived back at his flat.

'I went straight into the bedroom and began undressing whilst Mark locked up and paid a visit to the bathroom. I brushed my teeth and was laying naked on the bed reading a magazine when he came in with a mischievous look on his face. He also undressed and lay himself down beside me, letting out a little sigh of contentment when I reached down and grasped hold of his fast-swelling prick in my hand. When his shaft was at its fullest height I leaned over and wet my lips with my tongue, and I was just about to begin sucking his cock when I heard a noise from the hallway.

'"Mark, someone's just opened the front door," I whispered anxiously. "Ring the police, it must be a burglar." But Mark said soothingly: "Don't worry, darling, the noise came from upstairs. Old Mrs Kingsley always goes to play bridge on Thursdays and she's come back a little later than usual, that's all."

'"Are you sure?" I said, not fully convinced by this explanation. He sat up and swung his legs off the bed and said: "Look, I'll go and check and make sure all is well to put your mind at rest." I told him to be careful but he laughed and said that he was sure that no-one had come in. A minute or so later he returned and cuddled up next to me. "There, I told you the noise was from upstairs, you silly girl," he said, taking hold of my hand and wrapping my fingers around his erect prick. "Now, please feel free to continue what you had just started when we were disturbed."

'Well, I had no reason not to believe Mark and I heard no further noise from outside the bedroom, so I rubbed my hand up and down his shaft and leaned forward again and lapped all round the big purple knob, and then sucked in as much of his shaft as I could inside my mouth.

'"Aaah, that's divine, Tanya. You really must be the best little plater in London," said Mark and though I had never heard the word 'plater' before I guessed that he was complimenting me on my ability to perform, how do you say it, oral sex.

'Anyhow I closed my eyes and continued to suck Mark's thick penis, sliding my lips up and down his hot, stiff shaft, and slurping his bulbous knob along the roof of my mouth, all the way down to the back of my throat.

'Then again a noise disturbed me, but this time there was no doubt where it was coming from because I recognised the creaking of the bedroom door. I opened my eyes and to my astonishment saw Andrew Edwards and Charles Windsor standing by the door. So I had been right after all. I *had* heard someone come into the flat, and obviously Mark knew all about the arrival of these intruders. He could see I was angry but he placed his hands on my shoulders and said softly: "I'm sorry, Tanya, I should not have let Andrew and Charles in without telling you, but I couldn't resist showing you off to them and making them jealous."

'This apology cooled my anger but I was still cross with Mark for not asking me first if I minded fucking in front of other people. Actually, I had done so before at a party in Paris and I didn't mind all that much, especially when there were only two handsome young men like Andrew and Charles in the audience. So I thought to myself, I'll make you jealous, *mon brave*, so I tickled Mark's cock with the tip of my tongue and climbed on top of it, bouncing up and down on it till my pussy was sopping wet before reaching out and squeezing the big bulge which had swelled out in the front of Andrew's trousers.

'"Don't be shy, come and join in," I said and I don't think I have ever seen a man undress so quickly before! Seconds later he was kneeling on the bed beside me and I was looking at the biggest, stiffest prick I had ever seen in my life. It was so thick that I could hardly reach around it and it throbbed in my hand as I leaned over and sucked the huge knob into my mouth whilst continuing to slide up and down Mark's tool. Of course, Charles asked if he could join in, so I told him to take off his clothes and play with my breasts whilst I rubbed his cock with my left hand.

'Ah, *quelle experience!* I had Mark's penis in my pussy, Andrew's enormous cock in my mouth and Charles's prick in my hand. Mark came first, shooting his sperm in my cunt, and then Andrew filled my mouth with his spunk. He spurted so much jism that whilst I was swallowing it all down I did not notice that I was pointing Charles' cock towards Mark's face and, when Charles jetted his jism, the sticky white juice squirted into Mark's eye and splashed all over his hair. He had to retire to the bathroom to clean up and I noticed that Andrew's monster prick was still stiff as he stroked it in his hand.

'"I would love to fuck you, Tanya," he said and perhaps I looked a little scared as I stared at his enormous cock, for he continued in a gentle voice: "Please don't worry, I know that the size of my prick worries some girls. If you find it is too big for you, all you have to do is tell me and I will withdraw immediately."

'Well, I decided to find out for myself and parted my legs as he slowly slid his ruby knob inside my pussy. I was pleasantly surprised when he began to fuck me that such a big prick could move so gently inside me. He filled me completely as he thrust deeper and deeper, and I came twice before he exploded into me, flooding my cunt with a tidal wave of spunk.

'Poor Charles would have loved to have me but no girl could even think of having another prick inside her pussy after being fucked by Andrew Edwards. So I sucked him off instead and they left the flat shortly afterwards.'

Telling Ivor this erotic tale had excited Tanya, who now parted her legs invitingly, affording Ivor a close look at her dark, bushy thatch. 'Feel my pussy, it's all wet,' she purred as his hands smoothed their way up her bare thighs and then higher to rub her moist cunny. She threw back her head on the pillow as Ivor straddled her and buried his head between her legs and raked his tongue over the already erect little clitty. He slid his tongue between her pussy lips and probed inside her juicy cunt and, almost of their own volition, Tanya's legs splayed wider as she sought to open herself further to his questing tongue. He drew her love lips into his mouth and her hips thrust up in urgency as Ivor lapped up the love juice which was flowing freely from her cunny.

Unlike some of his friends, Ivor was always pleased to pleasure his sexual partners by eating their pussies, and he was in the seventh heaven of delight as his nose was assailed by the strong, tangy odour of Tanya's cuntal juices. Frantically, he attacked her clitty which trembled and twitched at his electric touch. She lifted herself from the pillow, jerking her hips upwards as her stiff little clit was drawn further and further forward between his lips and her hands pressed against the sides of Ivor's head as with a scream she climaxed and spurted a salty stream of love juice all over his mouth and chin until she sank down, sated by the delicious orgasm.

'Ah, Ivor, what a wonderful *hors d'oeuvres* – but what are you going to serve me for an *entrée*?' she asked cheekily as she released his head from its prison between her thighs.

'Whatever mademoiselle desires,' replied Ivor, clambering up on his knees. She smiled and opened her legs again and he mounted her, guiding home his rock-hard prick inside her aching pussy. Tanya now took over and, directing every inch of his sizeable shaft until it was snugly embedded in her cunt, she closed her thighs, making Ivor open his own legs and lie astride her with his throbbing tool well and truly trapped inside her clinging cunny.

Tanya gave a tiny growl of pleasure and then asked him: 'Are you comfortable? I love fucking in this position because I can feel every bit of your darling cock.'

'It's fine,' Ivor panted, though he could hardly pump in and out of her pussy as her cunny muscles were gripping him so tightly, although when she started to grind her hips, he sighed with delight as his penis was massaged exquisitely against the walls of her cunt. His penis began to pulse inside her juicy love channel and he sank his fingers into the cheeks of her soft bottom, inserting the tip of his forefinger into her bum-hole which made her squeal and wriggle in a new paroxysm of passion. She shifted her thighs and released his prick and, as the pressure eased, Ivor started to drive wildly in and out of her cunny, fucking at breakneck speed, the fierce momentum bringing Tanya off time and time again whilst he worked himself up to a magnificent climax. She brought her legs up against the small of his broad back, humping the lower half of her body upwards to meet the violent strokes from his raging cock. He bore down on her one more time, his body gleaming with perspiration, fucking her harder and harder, the rippling movement of his shaft playing against the velvety walls of her love channel and, as the end approached, he tensed his frame and with a cry crashed down upon her, his penis ejaculating spurt after spurt of spunk which streamed inside her slit as she quickly squeezed her thighs together and milked his spurting length, not releasing him until his prick began to shrink and he pulled it out of her slippery, wet crack.

A little later, as they sat naked in the kitchen drinking steaming hot mugs of coffee, Ivor explained that much as he would love to stay the day with her, he would have to leave after breakfast as he was catching the night train to Scotland that evening and there was some important work he had to do beforehand.

'But we will see each other as soon as you come back, I

hope?' said Tanya, looking at him with her large, liquid eyes, which melted any resistance Ivor might have felt to this request.

A vision of Julie fleetingly crossed his mind but he answered immediately: 'Of course! I won't be back till Thursday at the earliest, but perhaps we can see each other on Friday night.'

Tanya smiled as she rose up from her chair and scampered across to sit herself down on Ivor's knees. 'You will telephone me from Scotland, won't you?' she whispered as she nibbled the lobe of his ear. 'I will be here every night whilst you are away.'

'I'll call you tomorrow night without fail,' he promised and, as she cuddled his cock in her fist, he forced himself to add: 'Tanya, much as I'd adore another fuck, I really must be on my way.'

On his way back from Kensington Ivor wondered whether Julie had telephoned his flat late last night or, even worse, early this morning. She would be certain to think that he had already seduced another girl into his bed – well, she would be right, even though the gift had fallen so unexpectedly into his lap. He scowled as he remembered Brian Lipman telling him of a very apt phrase in Yiddish which the photographer's grandfather had been fond of using. Life was always *ober gur, ober gournisht*. There's always too much or not enough, Brian had translated as he bemoaned the fact that when he was busy, he was snowed under with work, but when things were quiet, the telephone would never seem to ring.

I never thought I would find myself with too many girls to satisfy, thought Ivor, strumming the steering wheel as he waited for the traffic lights to change at Marble Arch. Yet he had started two passionate relationships with Julie and Tanya and who knows whether Suzie would like to build upon the sensual tryst they had forged in Cable Publicity's boardroom? And what might happen if Tanya confided in her flat-mate that he had spent a feverish night of love-making in her bed?

Oh well, I could always become a monk, he ruminated, though this would be difficult as he was an avowed atheist. Or I could try turning queer, but that would be impossible as, though genuinely tolerant of what he considered a peculiar deviancy, he was too thorough a heterosexual to do anything but shudder at the thought of sexual play with another man.

In fact he had fibbed to Tanya as he had nothing to prepare for his journey that evening except to pack a small suitcase and, after he had completed this task, he read the *Sunday Pictorial*, noting with satisfaction as he scanned the Scottish football results that Aberdeen had trounced Kilmarnock seven-nil. Great, he said aloud, for he knew this would have made Willie McBain, an exiled Aberdonian who was a feature writer with one of the Glasgow evening papers, very happy. Ivor had met Willie on a previous trip to Glasgow and he considered whether there was an exclusive angle to the story which would ensure a good piece in the *Evening Star*.

He mentioned this to Brian Lipman when he saw him on the platform at Euston Station. 'It might be worthwhile, but let's face facts, it all depends how lucky we are,' shrugged the photographer. 'So long as there's no big news story like a royal visit, juicy murder trial or, God forbid, a plane crashing at Glasgow airport, I think we'll do okay.

'It'll all depend on the angles as the announcement of yet another new bloody dog food won't exactly make the editor hold the front page,' he said as they made their way down the carriage to their cabins, adding helpfully: 'Still, that's your job and I'm sure you've got some great ideas up your sleeve. You just tell me where to point my camera and I'll provide the pictures, so you'll have nothing to worry about on that score.'

He marched into his reserved accommodation and, after Ivor had dumped his bag in the adjoining sleeping berth, he went back inside and, with raised eyebrows, looked around the photographer's compartment which was twice as big as his own. 'How come you've twice as much space as me?' he demanded. 'Hey, there are two beds. They've given you a double berth by mistake.'

'No mistake, I need the extra room for all my gear and asked Suzie to book me a double berth,' said Lipman cheerily, clapping him on the shoulder. 'And don't worry, old love, I'll make it worth your while as far as the extra cost is concerned.'

'You mean you'll charge us twenty quid less for your photographs?' said Ivor quickly.

'Wash your mouth out! But you'll see, Ivor, it's a good investment, especially if the restaurant waitresses on duty tonight are anything like the air hostesses on my plane out to the States last April, or there could be a friendly group of girls going up to Scotland for a holiday. Come on, lock your cabin and I'll buy you a drink and give you the low-down on how to enjoy yourself on a long train journey. You've not travelled by sleeper before, have you?'

'No, last time we flew and a couple of years back I drove up with a couple of friends and we toured the Highlands,' said Ivor as he followed his colleague down the corridor to the bar. 'Some wonderful countryside there, Brian, you'd love it.'

Lipman ordered two large whiskies and brought them over to the table. 'Listen, what do you plan to do after dinner?' he asked as he passed one of the drinks over to Ivor. 'You want to read a book? Fine, I enjoy reading, but not more than for a couple of hours at a time. There's nothing else to do, though, Ivor – I know you've got more sense than to accept an invitation from anyone on the train for a friendly game of cards. And as you're not used to the noise, unless you sink a good few scotches, you'll find it damned difficult to get to sleep, even though the beds are comfortable enough.'

He looked around to make sure they would not be overheard and then leaned forward and said quietly: 'But for those who know, there are some very jolly parties that start up about midnight.'

Ivor stared at him in amazement. 'Are you pulling my leg?' he demanded, and was still only semi-convinced when Brian Lipman shook his head vigorously. 'No, honestly, you can have a great time on a sleeper if all goes according to plan.'

'Well, I've a bottle of scotch and a bottle of gin in my luggage,' grinned the photographer. 'And the girls bring along some ice and a few mixers from the bar. What more do you need?'

'But which girls are you talking about, Brian? I still don't understand you,' said Ivor who was only now taking in the idea that he might not sleep alone that evening.

'The odds are we'll meet some,' explained Lipman patiently. 'Of course there's no guarantee, but it's well worth being prepared if you happen to strike lucky.'

'And were you lucky on your last trip?'

'As a matter of fact, I wasn't,' Lipman admitted. 'But on the one before I scored with a history lecturer at Glasgow University. Look, I'll go and book dinner and when I come back we'll go over the programme for tomorrow and think of some gimmick which'll pull in the press. Then we'll have a bite to eat and survey any available talent. How does that grab you?'

'Sounds good to me,' said Ivor, taking out a notepad and fountain pen from his jacket pocket. 'I'll certainly be far happier if we can come up with an idea which will make the headlines.'

So he wasn't altogether displeased when Brian Lipman returned and, in far less excited tones, informed him that although he'd managed to reserve a table, the restaurant was staffed tonight solely by gloomy middle-aged waiters.

'Never mind, let's do some work, Brian. This is a bloody important job,' said Ivor unsympathetically to his disappointed colleague as the train lurched forward and slowly chugged its way out of Euston station. 'Just to recap, we're seeing this dog breeder, Mrs Rokeby, first thing tomorrow morning and we'll get the low-down on this mutt which she says always goes to the bowl with Four

Seasons, even if there's best chopped steak in two other bowls nearby.

'Then tomorrow, after we've met the press, you've arranged for two pretty Scottish lassies with playful, appealing little dogs on leads to walk along one of the main shopping streets handing out free sample tins of the stuff. Christ, you've remembered to bring the outfits, haven't you? Good, let's pray it doesn't rain. The girls must come along first to the press conference, of course, just in case the weather's bad and if the weather's okay, the photographers can go out with them into Sauchihall Street.'

'That's about it, Ivor. Now, who's the guy from Four Seasons we're meeting for breakfast at the hotel?'

'His name's Iain Taylor, and he's the Four Seasons company's Scottish area manager. He's been told to invite half a dozen or so selected buyers along to the press conference. Don't forget that you must get a few good pictures of them which we can send out to *The Grocer* and the trade press, and take a roll of colour so we can post copies to the buyers as souvenirs of their day out.'

'No problem. The only wee hiccup is that one of the girls I booked has cried off – she's got 'flu or some better job. Anyhow, Jimmy Campbell's agency is sending round two other girls at nine o'clock and I'll choose one of them to replace the girl who's dropped out. Don't worry, I've used Jimmy Campbell before, he won't let us down.'

'Well, that's covered all the bases,' sighed Ivor, swigging down a great gulp of scotch. 'What I'm looking for now is that gimmick which will make it all work.'

They sat in silence as the train rattled through Primrose Hill tunnel and gathered speed for the long haul up to Rugby, one of the few stations at which the express would stop on the four hundred mile journey to Glasgow. The steward came and invited them to take their seats for dinner, and he apologised to them as they entered the restaurant car, saying that there had been a sudden rush for tables, so would the gentlemen mind sharing a table for four with the two young ladies just up on the right hand side.

Brian and Ivor looked at the two pretty girls, one with a mop of red curls who was wearing a green mini dress which scarcely covered her buttocks, and the other a striking blonde girl who had taken off her jacket. Ivor caught his breath as his eyes fell upon the swell of her breasts which thrust out of a low-cut, tight cream blouse.

'Would that be all right, gentlemen?' asked the steward anxiously.

'Yes, of course, we don't mind at all,' said Brian Lipman heartily as he advanced upon the table with a gleam in his eyes.

I don't believe this, said Ivor to himself some ten minutes later. He had kept quiet as Brian Lipman had already established diplomatic relations with the two girls, who were both small-part actresses who had won minor roles in a new television detective series, an episode of which was being shot in Glasgow. 'We both play good-time girls who hang around Mister Big, a villain who the police don't manage to nab till the end of the series,' explained Beth Reynolds, the red-haired girl who had been delighted by Ivor recognising her from a TV commercial for a new beer.

'And who plays the bad guy?' asked Lipman.

'Jeff Wilson,' said the pneumatic blonde, whose name was Penny Glanville and who laughed heartily when the photographer said with interest: 'Then they couldn't have chosen a better Mr Big, could they? Tell me, is it true what they say about Jeff Wilson? I heard from an old mate of mine in the business that Jeff was a hell of a nice guy who happens to be exceptionally well-endowed, and that he's more than happy to swing his leg over any girl who wanted to see his enormous organ for herself.'

The girls exchanged a saucy look but shook their heads whilst Brian Lipman poured out champagne from the bottle he had ordered as they had sat down. 'Come on, girls, you don't have to be shy. Ivor and I can keep a secret,' urged the photographer, but at this stage the girls would say nothing more.

However, by the time the four had eaten the surprisingly good steaks and had finished a further bottle of champagne, as well as a bottle of Burgundy, the mood was very relaxed and, as they sampled the Napoleon cognac which the two men had insisted they should have with their coffee, Ivor asked again whether either had personal experience of Jeff Wilson's supposedly amazing prick.

This time Penny giggled and said: 'Well, if you must know, it isn't all that big and he isn't the greatest lover in the world. A few weeks ago I was standing at the bus stop outside my flat waiting to get to our rehearsal hall in Battersea. I was offered a lift by a couple of Hooray Henry types, but I would never accept a lift from a stranger.'

'Very wise of you,' commented Ivor, who was feeling rather tired and hot and he mopped some perspiration from his brow as he went on: 'Believe me, there are more nutters outside than inside these days.'

'And how! My young sister wanted to hitch a ride back to college in Birmingham, and I told her she must only try thumbing a ride if she could take a friend along with her. As it turned out, they met a nice couple of blokes, but that's another story.

'So there I was, waiting for the bus, and it was just starting to rain when a black, chauffeur-driven Jag purred up to where I was standing – and who should open the window but Jeff Wilson. "Hello there, Penny, I thought I recognised you – can I give you a lift?" he said and, as you can imagine, I was very pleased to see him! I could see him eyeing me up and down, especially my tits. I'm used to them being a bit on the big side and I must admit that I do try to show them off a bit. In our business, if you have it, you must flaunt it if you want to be noticed.

'Anyhow, when we arrived at the rehearsal rooms, one of the production secretaries came rushing out to tell us that our director and two senior members of the cast had gone down with food poisoning after eating at some grotty restaurant the previous evening, so that day's rehearsal would have to be cancelled. Jeff turned to me and said: "In that case, why don't we go back to my place and we can go through the little scene we have together? Then we can have a bite of lunch and find something else to do."

'You can imagine what he had in mind! The chauffeur took us back to Jeff's pad in Mayfair and we worked through the few lines we had to rehearse, and then we spent the rest of the morning listening to records (he's a great jazz fan) and simply lounging around, chatting about this and that. We went to the Mirabelle for lunch and I must say that I loved it when everyone stopped eating and stared at us when we marched in. A couple of people even came up and asked Jeff for his autograph. We had a lovely lunch and didn't get back to his flat till nearly half past three. I went into the bathroom and had a shower and came out twenty minutes later wearing just my crisp white panties. "My God!" he breathed as I sat down opposite him, draping my legs over the arms of the chair facing him and stretching my arms out behind me which made my naked breasts thrust out even more, and I could see that his eyes were glued to my big, pointy tits.

'We had drunk quite a lot at lunch but I could see a bulge forming in Jeff's lap as he stood up and threw off his jacket. He wrenched open his shirt and I glanced down and discovered that I was so wet for him that my panties already had a damp patch in the crotch. In a few moments Jeff was kneeling naked in front of me, positioning himself between my opened legs, fingering the outline of my pussy through my wet knickers. He kissed my nipples and I raised my bum so that he could pull down my panties, and then he started to beaver away between my thighs, parting my pussy lips with the tip of his tongue, and he found my clitty straight away and my bum cheeks squirmed around on the cushion as he started to flick my clitty from side to side with his tongue.

'"Fuck me, Jeff, fuck me with your cock!" I cried out when he began to slide two of his fingers in and out of my juicy cunny, and we held each other tightly as we rolled down onto the carpet. I was dying to see if what I'd heard about Jeff's cock was true, and so when I grabbed hold of his prick, I took a good look at it. Truthfully, it wasn't all that special. He's got one of those banana-shaped specimens, not all that thick but quite long. I gave it a rub and sandwiched it between my breasts which he liked very much. But I could see that Jeff was a bit tired to fuck very energetically so I pushed him onto his back and sat astride him, spreading the lips of my aching crack across his knob as I slowly sat down until his prick was fully inside me. I bounced up and down on top of his thighs and his hands slipped round to squeeze the cheeks of my bum.'

'Do you prefer being on top? Some girls swear by it whilst others don't like it at all?' said Brian Lipman.

'Oh, I love fucking that way,' said Penny promptly. 'I find it always gives my cunny walls a good pounding, and I can grind my bum around to make sure I give my clitty a good seeing-to as well – which is what I did with Jeff Wilson. I worked my bottom from side to side whilst he jerked his hips up and down. He couldn't hold back very long, though, and he spunked into me before I came, but he shot so much jism into me that it ran all down my thighs and soaked into the carpet. But Jeff was a considerate lover and when he realised that I hadn't come, he told me to lie back with my head against the chair and open my legs. We kissed and his hands cupped the undersides of my breasts and he brushed my tits with his hands as he held them between thumb and fingers, which I found very exciting.

'Then he looked straight into my eyes and winked at me before his head dived down and he started to munch my muff. Now Jeff's prick might have come too quickly for me, but he was a wonderful pussy eater. He drove his tongue right through my cunny lips and into my cunt, tossing it around the walls, withdrawing and plunging it in again, in and out, in and out, so quickly that at times there seemed to be no separation between his lips and my cunt. His hands now attacked my titties, flicking them up to hard little bullets as I trembled all over when the force of my oncoming orgasm began to surge through me.

'He stopped for a moment and raised his head as if to ask whether he should carry on. Of course I yelled at him: "Don't stop, Jeff, suck my clitty! Go on, suck it out!" And he did just that, managing to suck it in time with the waves of my orgasm and I came and came and came. Oh, it was marvellous, it makes me shiver just to think about it!'

There was a moment of silence before Beth patted Penny's hand and said: 'What a wonderful performance, darling, you had us all enthralled.'

'It wasn't a performance, Beth,' replied Penny indignantly. 'Those incidents really happened, I wasn't making anything up.'

'I'm sure you didn't, but you spoke so well that you had the audience in the palm of your hand,' said Ivor, who was now feeling very sleepy indeed. He stood up and announced: 'Sorry, folks, but you must excuse me. I'm feeling all-in and must lie down for a bit. Brian, be a good chap and see to the bill. I'll settle up with you later.'

Brian Lipman and the two girls chorused their sympathy and Ivor walked somewhat unsteadily back to his compartment. I'll be as right as rain after a little nap, he mumbled to himself, as he slid his arms out of his jacket which fell to the floor as he fell gratefully upon his bed and, within a minute, was fast asleep.

When his eyes fluttered open again about two hours later, Ivor blinked drowsily as his head slowly cleared – where the hell was he, and what was that clackety clack noise which at first he imagined had woken him up? Then his memory relayed the answers, though he caught his breath as a slight ripple of the bedclothes attracted his attention. He turned his head to see that sharing his bed, asleep and with her back towards him, was the slim, nude figure of Beth Reynolds, the pretty red-head who had been sitting opposite him during dinner.

He suddenly realised that he, too, was naked and peering across the small cabin he noticed that his clothes had been neatly folded across a chair. Beth stirred and swung her body over to face him.

She smiled and kissed his ear. 'Hello there, do you feel better now? Brian was quite worried about you but I thought you were simply over-tired and all you needed was a good rest. Am I right? Have you been burning the candle at both ends?'

''Fraid so,' admitted Ivor wanly as he heaved himself upwards to sit with his back pressed against the back of the bed. 'And just between ourselves, Beth, I'm bloody worried about whether our ideas for our client are going to turn up trumps in Glasgow.'

She also sat up and Ivor's eyes widened when her small, rounded breasts were revealed. His penis began to thicken when he gazed upon her nipples, tiny pointed rosebuds with large dusky pink areolae which begged to be kissed and caressed. Nevertheless, he continued to tell Beth about his concern about the publicity plans for an important client.

'We're making all the right noises – all we need is that one special gimmick which makes sure we make the papers,' he concluded, at the same time snuggling Beth into the crook of his shoulder. She frowned and tapped her fingers together as she thought hard about the problem, and then she exclaimed: 'Ivor, I've an idea which might do the trick. Tell me, Four Seasons couldn't do humans any harm, could it?'

'No, of course not, it's made from offal and God knows what from rabbits, poultry, whatever happens to be on the market at the time, although the stuff's genuinely highly nutritious for dogs. The firm making it has an excellent reputation. But why do you ask?'

She gave him a wicked smile. 'Well, you're throwing a reception for the press, aren't you? How about spreading a morsel of Four Seasons on a water biscuit and offering them round – no, better still, let the press see you and the guy from the manufacturer tucking in and licking your lips.'

Ivor looked at her with a mixture of admiration and horror. 'Christ, that's a wonderful idea, Beth, though I can't say I'm looking forward to trying it out. But what better accolade, eh? You clever girl!'

He grabbed hold of her in his arms and planted a firm kiss on her lips. Then, for some reason, he froze and their eyes locked into a deep pool of yearning and their mouths came together again in a deep, passionate kiss. Her supple lips rested on his for several moments and then Beth put her hands around his neck and pulled his face towards her. Her tongue met his and played inside Ivor's mouth and when their bodies crushed against each other, Beth gave a little gasp as she felt his hard, throbbing shaft sandwich itself against them. Her fingers explored the silkiness of Ivor's hair whilst his hands roved across her breasts before resting between her thighs as he kissed her chin and neck before he popped one of her jutting pink nipples into his mouth.

Beth threw back the covers and let her hand slide delicately up and down his hot, pulsating prick and Ivor trailed his forefinger all along her moistening hairy crack. He inserted the tip of his finger into her cunt and her muscles enclosed it like a vice, as if trying to squeeze fluid from it. She shuddered with desire as Ivor loomed over her and she helped guide his cock between her squelchy cunny lips deep inside her love channel, her fingers gripping his shaft as, looking down, she saw the bell-shaped bulb of his knob disappear between her wide-spread thighs. He entered her slowly in order to feel the ridge of his cock scrape along the walls of her cunt and he grunted with satisfaction as he felt the quiver of her little cunny muscles grabbing and relaxing whilst her hands reached round and clasped the cheeks of his dimpled bottom, pulling him into her as she moaned with joy, tossing her head from side to side as waves of pleasure rolled outwards from her saturated pussy.

He started to thrust forwards and backwards, spearing her in a quickening rhythm, and Beth raised herself to meet his rampant prick as he fucked her with rapid, pistoning strokes. He pounded in and out of her pussy and he rubbed her stalky nipples with one hand and snaked the other round to her backside to squeeze each luscious cheek in turn. She draped her arm around his neck, gasping and sobbing as, with a groan, Ivor spurted a warm, creamy fountain of spunk inside her and his spasms pushed Beth over the edge and she shrieked aloud when her climax sent electric tremors of ecstasy coursing throughout every fibre of her being.

Ivor rolled off the panting girl and lay next to her with his arm wrapped around her heaving body. 'God, that was wonderful, Beth. I hope the earth moved for you, too.'

She blew him a kiss and replied: 'Don't worry, Ivor, I'm not shy, if a man doesn't satisfy me, I'll soon let him know! Though I don't like being asked if I came – after all, any lover worth his salt wouldn't need to ask! But you asked whether I enjoyed myself as much as you and that's different – it shows that you consider my feelings as important as your own, which shows a caring nature.'

'I'm flattered, but you made things good for me by letting yourself go and not being afraid to take the initiative,' said Ivor. 'Believe it or not, we men sometimes worry about what we're expected to do next.'

'Yes, I'm afraid that many boys aren't sensitive enough when it comes to love-making,' sighed Beth softly. 'After all, anyone can stick their prick into a pussy. It isn't very difficult, is it? After all, sometimes I feel randy like just now and I want a cock to fill me as soon as possible. Then sometimes I like a cock to be put in a little at a time, do you know what I mean? First the tip and then the whole of the knob, very slowly in and out. The feeling of the ridge rubbing on my pussy lips is gorgeous! Then I'll want more and more, building up the tension until whoops, we're well away and we're shagging like crazy!

'But I'm concerned about you, Ivor. How about getting back to sleep? After all, it's only about eleven o'clock.'

'Is that all? God, I thought it was about six in the morning. No, I don't want to sleep any more, though it's lovely being in bed with you, Beth. I'm glad we have the rest of the night to find out more about each other,' said Ivor with relish. 'Honestly, I am so sorry about rushing away from the table at dinner. But I'm feeling fine now that I've had a good rest – and even more importantly, enjoyed a truly wonderful fuck!'

'Flattery will get you everywhere, you smooth-talking so and so,' she laughed, giving his flaccid cock a friendly tug. 'Tell you what, shall we pop next door and see how Penny and Brian are making out? I think they'd like to know that you've made a complete recovery.'

'Good idea,' agreed Ivor and he passed Beth his dressing gown whilst he slipped on a pair of pyjama trousers. Beth opened the door and looked carefully along the corridor to make sure the coast was clear. Then they hurried out and Ivor knocked on Brian Lipman's door. 'Open up, Brian, it's Ivor and Beth,' he called out and they waited impatiently until there was a click and the door opened a couple of inches. Ivor and Beth sidled in and saw the naked form of Brian Lipman climbing back into bed and resuming what he had been doing when Ivor had interrupted the proceedings. The photographer's rounded bottom was rising and falling between Penny's parted knees and from her gurgles of delight it appeared that the photographer was pumping away to good effect.

'Shoot your spunk, darling, I'm there!' came a muffled cry from Penny and Lipman increased the pace to a lightning speed and his body vibrated as, with a hoarse cry he jetted his jism inside her love channel whilst Penny threshed and writhed from side to side as the shuddering force of her climax swept through her.

The lovers dissolved into a tangle of glistening limbs and Lipman withdrew his deflated prick as they lay together, recovering from the fray. Beth turned to Ivor and remarked: 'I don't think we arrived at the most convenient moment, did we? Still, all's well that end's well, as Shakespeare would have said.'

'Yes, and as Gwendolen might have said in *The Importance Of Being Earnest*: "What a delight it is to share such a delightful fuck with a dear, new-found friend."'

There was a muffled yelp from the bed as Penny sat up. 'Oooh, I'm sorry, Brian, was I pressing your balls?' she apologised as she turned towards Ivor and Beth. 'Come on, I played Gwendolen when I was at drama school, and there's no such line in the play.'

'I didn't say there was,' replied Ivor with a grin. 'But did you know that some people now believe that Oscar Wilde wrote for *The Oyster*, one of the naughty underground magazines which flourished in the 1890s? There are a couple of very rude stories about Gwendolen and Cecily which appeared in *The Oyster* six months before the first night of *The Importance Of Being Earnest* in 1895. Of course, it was probably written by *The Oyster*'s editor, a guy called Lionel Trapes who was a close friend of Wilde, but the great man might well have added a few touches here and there to the manuscript. The magazine was very popular, but of course it was produced and sold secretly – not that the police would ever have prosecuted, there were too many Establishment people involved and the Prince of Wales was known to read every issue. I dare say the libraries at Buckingham Palace, the British Museum and the Vatican are the only places which still have copies.'

'The Vatican? I didn't know priests were supposed to read rude books,' said Beth.

'Some have to. It's their job to read all the new titles and see if they're fit for people to read. Anything risqué gets banned and is put on a list of banned books. It's said that the Vatican has the largest library of erotic books in the world.'

'How interesting! Where did you dig out all this information?' asked Beth curiously.

'The history of literature was one of my subjects at university,' Ivor explained, giving her a big cuddle. 'Now I don't know about you, but could we continue this lesson in bed? I'm getting rather cold standing here.

'That is, of course, so long as Penny and Brian don't mind moving up a wee bit,' he added politely.

'No, not at all, though it's just as well I booked a double berth, isn't it, Ivor?' said Brian Lipman with a note of triumph in his voice.

There was just enough room for the four of them to snuggle down and Ivor said: 'Tell you what, Penny, if you could write down some of your sexy adventures as stylishly as you told us about your day with Jeff Wilson, you'd make a fortune.'

She shook her head and said: 'I love telling a story and I don't feel at all embarrassed talking about sex, but I can't write things down. The fact is I'm slightly dyslexic, and I have problems learning my lines if I can't tape Beth or some other friend who'll be kind enough to read them for me. Luckily I have a very good memory so I've managed to struggle through so far.'

'Good for you, but that's quite a handicap for an actress,' said Ivor sympathetically. 'Still, I'm sure that *Playboy* would pay well for the piece, and I know that Brian would love to help you record them, wouldn't you, Brian?'

'I should say so,' said the photographer instantly. 'Ivor's right, you know, and I know some men's magazines in the States which would also offer big bucks for a picture spread to go with it.'

'Really?' said Penny with interest. 'I'm a performer and nudity is no big deal as far as I'm concerned. Ivor, you should know what Shaw wrote about it, as you're the English scholar. He said "all dress is fancy dress except we are in our natural skins" and if looking at my tits makes just one guy cream his jeans then I'm really pleased to have made somebody happy.'

'And you could also use the money,' added Beth with a

smile and Penny nodded: 'Sure I could, my car needs three new tyres! So please find out all the details for me, Brian, and we'll take things from there. We'll probably have to go through my agent, worse luck, as he gets fifteen per cent of my earnings, but he has brought in a lot of work this year so I suppose I shouldn't grumble too much.'

'Who are you with?' asked Ivor, who occasionally dealt with theatrical agencies when Cable Publicity needed a celebrity to open a supermarket or host a business conference.

'Clive Gradegate. Beth's with him, too. He's a young guy who was with one of the big agencies, but he broke away last year to set up on his own. He needs all the commission he can get so he works hard for us. Actually, there's a story about how he came to represent me. I'd been to the opening of a new night-club in Soho and we started chatting at the bar. Clive told me how he was planning to break away from Newman's and start his own business, and he asked me if I was happy with my agent, Lou Baum of Dyott's.

'Well, Lou knew lots of people but he hadn't been doing much for either Beth or me, and I said that though I couldn't speak for Beth I would imagine that we might both be interested in signing up with a new agent who would try his best for us. "I'll do that," he promised and after we downed a few drinks, he took me out to the dance floor. I love dancing and I didn't know that Clive started his career in show business as a chorus boy. It was magic jiving with him, and I was sorry that the party ended early.

'Clive drove me back to our flat and I invited him in for coffee. It was rather late but Beth was away that night so I thought it would be nice if I switched on the radio and we could continue dancing. But at this time of night, the music coming from the radio was soft and smoochy and I was so relaxed by now that I draped myself against him. In no time I was returning his kisses and thrusting my hips up against the swelling bulge in his trousers.

138

'I stiffened when I felt his hand tug down the zipper of my dress but Clive was as good a kisser as he was a dancer. His hands pulled the dress free of my shoulders and it dropped to my waist. Then his hands went round my back and unhooked my bra which fell down to the floor. He bowed his head and began to lick my nipples which drove me wild and my whole body shook with lust as he made his way from one quivering globe to another. Honestly, I became so weak at the knees that I thought I might faint.

'"Where do you sleep?" he asked softly and I jerked my head towards the bedroom. He picked me up in his arms and tenderly lay me down on the bed. "Aren't you going to join me?" I enquired, holding out my arms to him, and he smiled gently and said: "Only if you want me to, Penny, I wouldn't want you to think I would try and bully you into anything – and incidentally, that's the way I would work business-wise if I represented you and your friend."

'"Well, I like the sound of that, Clive," I said, lifting my hand up to unzip his fly. "And I'd also like to see what personal services you can offer me on an exclusive basis." I fished inside his trousers and brought out his cock and, wow! He was circumcised with an immense, very thick shaft which throbbed excitedly in my hands. Okay, I know that size isn't everything but a big, juicy pole like Clive's would make any girl drop her drawers.

'He undressed and his lithe, muscular body was soon hovering over me. I closed my eyes in ecstasy as I felt the tip of his huge, rounded knob slip lightly between the lips of my pussy. I gasped with delight, clinging frantically to him, and my legs flew up in the air as he sank his great shaft to depths that I didn't even know I possessed. I clung on for dear life as he pistoned his prick in and out of my sopping cunt, my nails clawing at his back and at his firm buttocks which were rising and falling over me. He was fucking me so beautifully that I was coming time and time again, each time I lifted my hips upwards in rhythm with his thrusting downward plunges.

'When I finally exploded into a tremendous final orgasm, I screamed and began bucking my hips, carrying him high off the bed, and I nearly fainted when he drove even deeper and his swelling cock started to spurt inside my honeypot.

'This was such a glorious fuck that I wanted more! So I slid my hand down to his shaft to see whether Clive was ready to continue, but my pussy had drained him so completely that his prick remained limp, even when I took his sweet knob in my mouth and washed it all over with my tongue. I tried to conceal my disappointment but Clive could sense that I needed more love-making, and he said apologetically: "Sorry, Penny, but I'm afraid that my John Thomas always requires at least twenty minutes between performances. But tell me, did you hear the story of the chap who only had a two-inch cock but who always had a queue of girls waiting to jump into bed with him?"

'I giggled and said no, and Clive smiled and said: "Well, one day his best friend who was very well endowed came round and asked him how he managed to attract so many women. 'Ah,' said the guy, 'that's because I can lick my eyebrows!'"

'This made me laugh out loud and then we kissed long and passionately, my body gyrating with desire as Clive ducked his head down and his tender mouth enveloped my nipples, one after the other, sucking gently which made me cry out with pleasure. He moved his lips slowly across my tummy, all the time kissing me softly with his lips and tongue until he came to the edges of my blonde bush. I parted my thighs because I thought he was going to bury his head between them and suck my pussy, but I was wrong. He continued kissing me all the way down to my feet, all the while caressing my body with a practised expertise.

'Then he took my foot in his hands and kissed my toes, moving his tongue sensually between them. This was a wonderful turn-on and I writhed and twisted from side to side, for my cunny was tingling and my clitty had already popped out of its hood. Oh, I could hardly wait for him to reach it!

'At last he heaved his body upwards between my legs, turning his head to kiss the inside of my knees, and then he spread my thighs apart and ran his fingers up to my pulsing pussy. Lightly opening my love lips he pressed his mouth against my cunt and when I felt his warm breath, shivers of delight ran through me and I bucked and humped into his face, wrapping my legs around his shoulders, trying to let his tongue slide even deeper into my juicy crack. He lapped eagerly at the love juice which was running freely out of my cunt and I felt an enormous orgasm building inside me as I arched up to meet his mouth and he began to finger-fuck me very quickly, stabbing two fingers in and out of my cunny whilst he licked me out. This brought me up to a lovely climax and I quivered into a crescendo of waves and waves of luscious orgasms.'

At this point, Penny paused and looked down at Ivor and Brian's cocks which were both bolt upright and turning to Beth. She licked her lips and said: 'Darling, telling this story has made me terribly randy. Would you be very upset if Ivor fucked me?'

'No, of course not, help yourself,' said Beth generously, making a fist with her fingers to rub briskly up and down Ivor's erect member. 'His prick's good and ready for you, darling.'

'H'm, that's a nice-looking specimen,' said Penny, replacing Beth's hand with her own. 'Now let's find out if it tastes as good as it looks.'

She wriggled down the bed until she had brought her head level with Ivor's palpitating prick, bringing her lips level with the uncapped purple knob. She let her tongue run down the veiny length and then back up again to the tip to catch a hot, sticky drip of jism which had already formed around the tiny hole in the mushroomed dome. She ran her lips over the rounded helmet and then opened

141

her mouth as instinctively Ivor jerked upwards and forced at least four inches of his succulent shaft between her lips. Worried in case he choked the sweet girl, Ivor retracted slightly and let his tadger lie throbbing on her tongue. She closed her mouth around its girth, moving her tongue across its width, and Ivor let out a strangled cry of ecstasy as Penny sucked greedily on his bursting tool.

Brian Lipman now tried to join the action but Beth pulled his prick backwards and whispered for him to wait. She sat herself down next to Penny and inserted her forefinger through the blonde pussy bush into her friend's moist honeypot. Penny wriggled on the intruding finger as the walls of her love channel contracted around it.

'Ooooh, that's marvellous, Beth,' she breathed throatily. 'Now be a good girl and make me come!'

For reply Beth jerked her fingers in and out of Penny's sopping, silky muff as she moved her head between her thighs and started licking her pussy, which sent the pretty blonde into fresh tremors of ecstasy as she continued to bob her head up and down Ivor's glistening shaft, and the red-haired girl turned to Brian Lipman and muttered wickedly: 'I'll tongue Penny till her pussy will be craving like mad for your cock. She simply adores to have her cunt licked from her clitty to her bum. Look, I'll show you what I mean.'

Sure enough, Penny's legs threshed around wildly as Beth now diddled her cunny and sucked on her hard little clitty whilst she slipped her free hand between her own legs to frig herself at the same time. This erotic scene so excited Brian Lipman that the photographer could not wait to find out whether or not Beth was right. With his stiff cock sticking up high in the air, the photographer shuffled across on his knees and placed himself behind Beth. He manoeuvred her hips upwards until the delicious cheeks of her bottom were pouting outwards as he parted them with his hands and slid his pounding prick into the crevice between the soft, fleshy spheres. He let it stay there for a few moments before withdrawing his tool, then wet his helmet with saliva before aiming his knob directly at the wrinkled little rosette of her bum-hole.

He eased into her slowly but firmly, sliding his smooth bell-end between Beth's magnificent buttocks which looked fairly aching to be split. He pushed forward and his shaft was soon enveloped in between the in-rolling cheeks of her beautifully proportioned backside and, when he was fully inside the tight sheath, Lipman started to work himself backwards and forwards with vigour, making Beth's bum slap against his belly as she wriggled lasciviously whilst keeping her lips glued to Penny's sopping pussy.

'God, what a wonderful bum-fuck!' he panted as he leaned over Beth to fondle her rosy tipped breasts and play with her hard, erect nipples.

Ivor was the first to come, filling Penny's mouth with fierce spurts of spunk which she gulped down as his cock twitched violently in her mouth. This brought on Penny's climax and Beth lapped and swallowed her salty spend as a fountain of love juice gushed out of her sopping cunny. Almost immediately Brian Lipman flooded Beth's backside with such vibrant squirts of sperm that the photographer swore that he could actually see the ripples of orgasm running down her spine as she shuddered to a tremendous orgasm. As she artfully wiggled her bottom, he ejaculated spout after spout of creamy jism into her arse-hole until with a 'pop', he withdrew his still turgid tool from her and sank back on his haunches. Beth turned round with a shining face and bent her head down to suck his wet shaft, gobbling down the last drains of spunk until his thick, glistening penis slowly began to deflate.

The lustful quartet lay panting with fatigue and Brian Lipman could only groan when Penny turned to him and said brightly: 'Isn't it time that you found out how juicy my pussy is, Brian?'

'You must be joking,' he protested weakly. 'I'm out for the count, my girl – well, at least for half an hour or so.'

She looked at Ivor who put up his hands in a gesture of surrender. 'Sorry, love, but I'm all-in too!'

'Dear me,' said Penny with mock severity as she smoothed her hand between her legs. 'My cunny is still all wet and juicy. I need to be finished off, but neither of you boys seem able to rise to the occasion. Who said that women are the weaker sex? Beth, I need you and our little friend which you'll find in the usual place.'

Ivor and Brian exchanged puzzled glances as Beth leaned over the side of the bed and rummaged in Penny's handbag. Meanwhile, Penny lay on her side, facing the boys, her fingers tenderly parting the moist, golden hairs around her prominent pussy lips, and then her hand was firmly pushed aside from behind her by Beth, who continued this insistent frigging by caressing the delicate white flesh of Penny's thighs which quivered under her touch. Then Beth ran her forefinger along the length of her long slit whilst the two girls kissed, like sisters at first, but then with parted lips, their pink tongues curling together as their mouths eased away from each other, leaving them free to lick provocatively, making contact with just the tips of their tongues.

Beth now closed her left hand upon Penny's golden cunt and lay the trembling girl on her back as she mounted her. In her right hand she held a thick, rubber, ribbed dildo of a kind neither Ivor nor Brian had seen before, for both ends were fashioned like the knobs of huge, stiff penises. She flashed a quick look to the men and said: 'Haven't you two ever seen a Black Mamba before? No? Well, Penny and I will show you how they work.'

She pressed one end gently against Penny's pussy lips which instantly opened to take in the rubbery imitation prick, which Beth worked into her honeypot until her love-channel was completely filled. Then Beth pulled herself up until she was sitting on the blonde girl's thighs. Their eyes locked as Beth vibrated the dildo inside Penny's pussy with one hand whilst, with the other she rubbed her fingers along her own wet gash, and when her cunny had moistened up she raised herself up and pushed the free end of the Black Mamba between her own love lips.

Penny wrapped her arms around her friend and pulled her downwards until the girls were pressed tightly together, breasts to breasts and cunt to cunt. Ivor and Brian watched in quiet fascination as the dildo squelched in and out of the two girls' cunnies as they jerked their hips to and fro along its cock-sized double knobbed shaft. They squealed with pleasure as they rocked back and forth and the girls soon achieved a delicious rhythm as they fucked themselves on this imitation prick.

Their motions became more and more frenzied as their excitement grew, and Beth now pushed Penny flat on her back and stretched out her body across her friend with the heads of the dildo still clamped firmly inside their sticky, suctioning pussies. Penny grabbed Beth's jutting breasts and frantically rubbed her large red nipples against the palms of her hands as her body convulsed and her head thrashed from side to side on the pillow. 'Oh, Christ Almighty, that's wonderful! Don't stop now, Beth darling, don't stop! Oooh, Oooh, Oooh! Yes, I'm almost there!' she shrieked as her heels drummed madly on the mattress.

Of course Beth had no intention of stopping and kept fucking her juicy cunny as well as her own with their rubber cock, and she continued to remorselessly rock to and fro, her tousled head thrown back, her neck arched forward, her shoulders shaking. They were lost in each other, each spurred on by an intensity which locked their bodies as their breathing quickened and their bodies twisted and turned. Then with loud cries of fulfilment the two girls climaxed almost together, with tangy rivers of love juice streaming out of their cunnies and onto the sheets, which were already well stained from the quartet's previous exertions.

'My goodness, that'll be a hard act to follow,' murmured Brian Lipman, and Ivor nodded his head sagely as the two girls lay heaving and panting in each other's arms.

'I don't know whether I'm up to it yet,' added Ivor but, fortunately for the two men, Penny and Beth were more interested in some hot coffee and a tot of Chivas Regal which Lipman had thoughtfully stowed away in his luggage.

Still naked, they sat on the bed, and as she tested the delightfully smooth whisky, Beth suddenly said: 'This party reminds me of something very strange which happened to me quite recently to do with a train journey. If I tell you about it, will you promise not to laugh?'

'Scout's Honour. You won't even see any of us smile, will she, chaps?' said Ivor, settling himself down with his head in Penny's lap as the blonde girl and Brian Lipman chorused their approval. 'So go on, Beth, you have the floor.'

She twiddled her glass between her fingers and paused for a moment before saying: 'Well, don't forget your promise, I'll be really cross with anyone who makes fun of me about anything afterwards.

'It happened three weeks ago to the day. Beth, you might remember that you had gone down to Bourne-mouth that weekend to see your parents.'

'Sure I do,' trilled Beth lightly. 'And I also remember how it worked out very nicely because you had a Saturday night dinner date with that nice young guy from Associated Television casting, Mike Harper, and you told me it was most convenient that I was going to be away as you wanted him to stay over through to Sunday.'

Beth nodded and went on? 'Mike was a wonderful lover and we stayed in bed till lunchtime. "I'm going to get up and make us a bite to eat," I announced, but he pulled me back and whispered in my ear: "Don't bother, Beth, we'll go out for lunch, but first, let's have one final fuck."

'I didn't need much persuading and as I ran my fingers through his thick, curly hair I could feel my pussy getting wetter and wetter whilst his mouth explored every nook

146

and cranny of my body. I trembled all over as I offered him my breasts and he played with my titties, and I stroked his rigid prick as he moved his body over mine.

'We'd made love all night and I was more than ready for his swollen shaft which he slid between my pouting love lips and, as he fucked me, his balls banged against my bum. I wrapped my legs round his back and straight away he began slewing his big, circumcised cock in and out of my dripping honeypot. We rocked together in perfect rhythm and I was blissfully enjoying the gorgeous tingling sensations in my cunt when suddenly – and you'll find this difficult to believe – I heard a woman's voice as clear as a bell saying to me in a broad Scottish accent: "Beth, don't forget now, you're meeting me at Euston at half past two."

'Obviously Mike had not heard it because he was still pounding his prick in and out of my cunny, but he felt my body tense and he let about three inches of his pulsating pole stay still in my cunt as he said: "Beth, what's the matter? Did I push in too hard?'

'"No, no, I was loving it," I said quickly, squeezing my thighs around his stiff tadger. "But I heard someone give me a message – didn't you hear some woman speak?" He looked at me in astonishment and shook his head. "You must be dreaming, darling," he said and slowly began to move his twitching tool back and forth. "My cock must have sent you to dreamland. Come on, we've started so we'll finish."

'I must be going potty, I thought to myself, but I tried to forget what I had heard and concentrated on Mike's marvellous penis which was now flashing in and out of my creamy pussy. "I'm going to fill your pussy to the brim with spunk," he panted and just as I felt the first spatterings of his jism splash against the walls of my cunt, would you believe it, I heard the voice again. This time she said: "Och, you dinnae have to worry, lass, we've been held up at Bletchley and the guard's just told us we'll be stuck here for at least twenty minutes."

'Mike's frame shuddered as he shot his load and slicked his quivering cock in and out of my cunt until his prick began to shrink. He looked at me and said tenderly: "Love, you didn't come then, did you? What's wrong? Have you been hearing strange voices again?"

'Then suddenly it hit me – I *was* supposed to meet someone at Euston – my Great Aunt Rosie who lives in Manchester, but surely she was coming next week . . . I told Mike and I jumped out of bed and ran across the room to grab my diary which was sitting on the dressing table. I opened it up and I nearly fainted when I saw that I had made a mistake and Great Aunt Rosie was indeed coming to London this afternoon!

'Now of course I recognised her voice because, although she's been living in Manchester for the last fifty years, she was born and bred in Edinburgh and she's never lost her accent.

'My head was spinning and I put my hand down on the dressing table to steady myself. Mike, bless him, leaped out of bed and steadied me, leading me over to a chair. I slumped into it and then he said gently: "Just tell me quietly what you heard."

'After I had explained everything, he declared: "Come on, Beth, let's get some clothes on and I'll run you up to Euston straight away."

'I looked at him gratefully and said: "Mike, that's kind but there's no great rush, she said the train will be twenty minutes late." But he pooh-poohed this, saying that however strangely this had entered my stream of consciousness, the fact of the matter was that the train was scheduled to arrive at half past two.

'Well, we showered and dressed ourselves and Mike made me gulp down a tot of brandy because he told me that I looked as white as a sheet and truthfully, I was indeed still feeling pretty ropey from the whole peculiar business. We arrived in good time at Euston, a little after a quarter past two. I wanted to stay in the car but Mike opened the door and offered his arm. "The fresh air will do you good," he said as we walked over to the information desk. I held on tightly as Mike asked the clerk if the Manchester train due at half past was on time, and the man shook his head. "I'm sorry, sir, the train's running twenty minutes late, there's been a derailment just outside Bletchley."

'Even Mike paled at this and I felt a tremor pass through his body as I clutched his arm. "Let's go for a drink," he suggested and we sat in silence, nursing our whiskies whilst we waited for Great Aunt Rosie to arrive.

'When her train finally chugged into the station we walked along the platform and soon spotted my Great Aunt who was already off the train and was peering through the crowd to look for me. "Hello, Beth, how lovely to see you," she cried as I ran up to her, and she gave me a big kiss on my cheek as I introduced Mike to her. "You know, I'm getting to be a silly old woman, we had just passed through Crewe when it suddenly struck me that you might have forgotten you were meeting me, for it's three weeks since I wrote to you to say I was coming down to London for a few days to stay with my old friend, Mrs Macdougall."

'"Were you really worried, Auntie?" I said, looking purposefully across at Mike. "Very wrong of me, I know," she confessed. "And then when we were stuck outside Bletchley, I thought to myself, well, even if Beth only remembers to meet me at the last minute, it won't matter if she's late because we won't be at Euston till almost three o'clock."

'I said nothing more except to laugh and, without a blush, I chivvied her for thinking I could be so scatter-brained as to forget to turn up to meet her, and we dropped Great Aunt Rosie at Mrs Macdougall's house in Barnes. Mike and I didn't speak much as we let Auntie Rosie chatter on, but Mike was uncharacteristically quiet on the way back to the flat.

'"Are you feeling okay?" I asked him and he said, sure, he was feeling fine. So I suggested that we go back to bed and complete some unfinished business. But do you know, Mike had been so affected by what had happened that he couldn't perform any more. There we were, lying stark naked on the eiderdown, and I simply couldn't make his cock stiff! I tried rubbing it, licking it, sucking it but his prick would only swell up for a few seconds before going limp again. Naturally, he became all panicky, but I told him that an occasional failure to perform meant nothing, especially in these circumstances. Of course, he found this difficult to accept as he had never suffered from this before, but I think in the end I managed to persuade him to forget all about it till our next date on the following Wednesday night.'

Penny shivered and said: 'You never told me about this before, Beth. No wonder Mike looked so unhappy when I came back from Bournemouth later that afternoon.'

'Sorry, darling,' Beth apologised, squeezing her hand. 'I didn't want to say anything in case you might think I was going crazy!'

'I don't think you're in the slightest bit crazy, Beth,' said Ivor forcefully and Brian Lipman echoed his friend's opinion. 'Mind you,' the photographer added darkly. 'Believe me, at some time or another we all come across something or other which seems to defy understanding.'

Unknown of course to any of them, by an extraordinary coincidence, these very same words had been uttered about an hour before in the adjoining compartment by a stunning young blonde named Wendy Oakridge whilst she was frantically sliding her closed fist up and down the sizeable but flaccid penis of the Honourable Antony Godfrey, the son of Viscount Greencroft of Kenton, a sharp-witted North London businessman who had amassed an enormous fortune from selling Government surplus after World War Two. A marriage into an impoverished but blue-blooded Shropshire family, and a shrewd penchant for making substantial donations without fear or favour to the favoured charities of whichever Prime Minister happened to be in power, led first to a knighthood and then a viscountcy for the portly little man who had left school at fifteen years of age to start work in his parents' wholesale grocery in Finsbury Park.

To the fury of the Viscount, his sole son (whose birth had been much welcomed after his wife had produced four daughters) possessed few of the qualities which had propelled Harold Godfrey to the top. Antony had always shown talent as a scholar and as a sportsman – at Cambridge University he had gained a lower second class degree in the history of art and had won blues for cross country running, fencing and soccer – yet he admitted to an indolent disposition and told his despairing father that, frankly, as he had the luck to be born with a silver spoon in his mouth, he was going to spend his time solely in the pursuit of pleasure and make the most of his good fortune.

And what good fortune! For what further angered his father to the point of apoplexy was that to avoid paying huge amounts of income tax, when Antony was three years old, Viscount Greencroft set up an irrevocable trust solely in favour of his son which, thanks to careful management, had swelled to more than two and a half million pounds by the time Antony was twenty-five and under the terms of the trust, inherited this amount which, to Viscount Greencroft's fury, left him free of all parental control.

This made Antony Godfrey very unpopular with his father, who no longer had the power of the purse strings to make Antony settle down to do a full day's work, and it was of little comfort that his son was the toast of Fleet Street gossip writers for, on a poor news day, they could usually rely on a story about Antony Godfrey to fill the diary page.

There were two reasons why this was so – firstly, Antony had inherited one filial attribute. He was noted for his generosity with his cheque book though, unlike his father who had calculated the benefits from supporting any particular cause, Antony enjoyed giving for the sake of giving to any and all individuals, organisations and causes which took his fancy. Antony was also a prodigious ladies' man and girls swarmed around his bulky frame (for he had inherited his father's physique) although even now at the age of thirty-two he showed no signs of wanting to settle down and get married.

And what of the girl who had echoed Brian Lipman's words about there being some things which seemed 'to defy understanding'? Wendy was a stunning girl of nineteen who was desperate to further her career as a folk singer. She looked well enough on stage, sitting on a stool with the long, shining strands of golden hair falling down over her face as she picked out the chords on her somewhat battered guitar, but a recording contract had eluded her, perhaps because she would only sing authentic folk music and, though her voice was tuneful enough, producers believed that mournful warblings about the pitiful state of the world would not make the charts.

But Wendy was determined to stick with her principles and, to make ends meet in the big city, she found a job as a waitress at Little Ron's, a Soho coffee bar patronised by people working in the music industry in nearby Denmark Street, or Tin Pan Alley as it was known in the business, where she would also sing for an hour in the evenings. Some three weeks afterwards Antony Godfrey and one of his friends had popped into Little Ron's one evening and the rich philanthropist fell hook, line and sinker for the waif-like, coltish blonde who was singing an Elizabethan love ballad with such dramatic feeling through a background buzz of conversation in the half-empty café.

He had invited her back to his table and his companion tactfully made his farewell when it became plain that Antony had been smitten by the good-looking girl. They struck up a genuine friendship from the first moments of introduction and that night he ran Wendy back home to her bedsit in Camden Town. She was flattered by the attention of a wealthy, slightly older man and enjoyed the minor fame of being photographed in a night club and seeing her face appear in the newspapers as 'the pretty companion of fun-loving Antony Godfrey, shown dancing the night away', but being wined and dined in the best places meant little to Wendy, for she was as consumed with the burning ambition to succeed as a folk singer as much if not more than Antony was determined not be become involved with any matter which might affect his hedonistic life-style.

Although by nature Wendy was a passionate, sexy girl who had only a month before finished a six-month relationship with a boy from her hometown of Luton, much to his disappointment Antony was allowed at best half an hour's heavy petting after he had brought her home after a date. He had felt like a fifteen-year-old again when, after managing to slip his hands inside her blouse and unhook her bra, Wendy had refused to let him do more than caress her small, uptilted breasts. When he had slid his hand under her skirt or attempted to pull her hand down to feel his bursting stiff prick, she pulled away, saying that she was not ready yet to sleep with another man and he would have to show patience.

Then it struck him that the quickest way to her heart (and other parts of her body!) would be to try and further her career. Without telling Wendy of his plan, he managed to persuade Benny Dunn, the highest-flying Artists and Repertoire man in London, to spend an evening at Little Ron's, but the record producer was not greatly impressed. 'The girl looks good and her voice is fairly distinctive,' Benny had said bluntly. 'But she needs a good manager and preferably a singing coach to bring out the best in her.

'Tell you what though, Tony, the man who could help you is a guy named Kent Webster who puts on folk and country music concerts all over Europe. He's the most powerful person in the folk business and if he took her on board, then I think she could go places. Look, if you want to contact Kent, he'll be in Glasgow for the next two weeks auditioning for a big Folk Festival there early in the New Year. My company is going to make some live recordings from the Festival so I'm in touch with Kent all the time. Would you like me to see if I can get him to listen to Wendy?'

Antony gratefully accepted Benny Dunn's kind offer and the next day told Wendy all about it. Not surprisingly, she had been tremendously excited when he told her that Benny had fixed an appointment for her to see Kent Webster the following Monday at noon in Glasgow. But then her pretty face had creased up into a frown. 'I can take some time off, no problem,' she had said to him. 'But getting to Scotland and staying in Glasgow might be a bit difficult. I haven't any friends up there, and I can't afford to stay in a hotel.'

'Don't be daft, I'll take you up on the Sunday night train,' he had said, and her eyes had sparkled and she had thrown her arms round his neck and kissed him. 'I'll book a nice double for us on the sleeper,' he had added and, to his delight, Wendy had not baulked at the idea and he had booked the tickets that same afternoon.

But as Murphy's Law so eloquently states, if anything can go wrong, it will, even though Wendy had made no comment when the porter hauled their cases into their compartment. They had sat opposite the table where Ivor and Brian were talking animatedly to Penny and Beth, and when Ivor had left the table and stumbled out of the restaurant car, Wendy had massaged the side of his calf with her foot and had whispered: 'I think that chap's had a bit too much to drink. You go easy on the brandy now, Tony. I don't want you suffering from brewer's droop this evening.'

Antony Godfrey had heeded her advice and, after he had paid their bill, the couple made their way back to their quarters. He locked the door and pulled off his jacket before taking the nineteen-year-old blonde beauty in his arms and crushing her in a passionate bear hug, smothering kisses all over her pretty, freckled face.

154

'Let's undress,' he growled and she smiled roguishly. 'Last one on the bed's a cissy,' she teased and giggled naughtily when Antony almost tripped over his own feet in his eagerness to tug down his trousers. He was lying naked on the bed almost before she had rolled down her tights, and when she stood nude except for her frilly blue panties, he sat up and, with trembling hands, pulled down the tiny garment, for the first time feasting his eyes on the thick, corn-coloured bush which surrounded the pouting pink lips of her pussy.

Wendy let her lips pass slowly over her top lip and let herself be pulled down on top of him as Antony turned on to his side and pressed her compliant body into the crescent of his own warmth. Wendy let herself be carried away as their lips met and their mouths opened, and she felt a glorious wave of sensual energy hurtle through her as his hands roamed freely over her body. He kissed her pointed nipples which had swelled to two little red peaks and she gasped as his fingertips ran along the edges of her cunt, and she reached down to squeeze his penis which until now had remained a hard, hidden bulge in his lap.

Yet when her fingers found his prick, to her amazement she found the thick, circumcised shaft still limp, hanging forlornly over his thigh. Sensibly she said nothing but wondered what she should now do. Although she had only slept with three other men, she had been petting since she first played Postman's Knock at her friend's fourteenth birthday party when she had let Richard Pearce slip his hand inside her blouse whilst they kissed, and she had swiftly rubbed her hand against the bulging pole in his trousers which was trying to flatten itself against her. Since then she had seen and played with a variety of pricks of different shapes and sizes, but all had risen to a throbbing stiffness by the time she had touched them.

Meanwhile beads of perspiration had formed on Antony's forehead. 'I'm sorry, Wendy, I don't know what's happened,' he murmured fearfully. 'I've had a hard-on almost since we boarded the train, but as soon as I undressed my cock just collapsed like a burst balloon.'

'Try not to worry, you're just over-anxious, that's all,' replied Wendy softly as she nibbled his ear. Then she deftly shifted her body so that she lay on top of him and kissed his nipples before sliding her mouth down to his flat, hard-muscled belly and into the crinkly, dark hairs which ringed his flaccid shaft.

Half angry and half amused at the plight of his soft, vulnerable penis which twitched feebly in her hand, Wendy lowered her head and licked all around the edges of the smooth, mushroom-shaped knob. She tickled the sensitive underside with the tip of her tongue and now his anxiety communicated itself to her as she realised that even this stimulation was not working.

She ruffled his hair with her hands and then he turned and his arms enveloped her, his body curling around hers like a protective covering. Antony immediately fell into a deep sleep, but Wendy was not yet ready to close her eyes and she carefully disentangled herself from his warm embrace and replayed what had just happened in her mind. She had read in the problem pages of women's magazines how men sometimes found that their sexual organs played terrible tricks upon their owners. Yet Antony had been so eager to possess her, and now, when at last she had yielded, for some odd reason he had been unable to accept the freely offered gift!

But in heaven's name, why? Wendy sighed and told herself that this little business was simply one of those matters which defied any logical understanding and there was no point brooding about it. She was not feeling sleepy and so she decided to read the paperback novel Antony had bought at the station bookstall. The book was lying on top of his case which was near enough for her to be able to stretch out an arm and pick it up. However, as she lifted the paperback, two sheets of notepaper which had been folded inside the pages fluttered out onto the bed which were covered with Antony's writing.

To her surprise, when she glanced at one of the sheets, Wendy noticed that she was reading a letter which was addressed to her! 'What the hell are you up to, Antony?' she murmured softly, and she was about to put back the letter on his case when she suddenly decided that as it was meant for her eyes, it would hardly be a breach of trust if she took a quick peep before Antony himself actually gave it to her.

She sat up and read:

My darling Wendy,

I planned to give you this letter before we make love on the train, but I felt strangely shy about even writing it and so I have waited till we are together in our suite at the hotel.

I'm not usually tongue-tied but I've found it difficult to express my feelings towards you and so, because I want you to know how I feel about our relationship, I'm scribbling this billet-doux at half past two in the morning in order to vent these heartfelt, pent-up emotions which at present are churning around in my brain.

You must realise how much I have desired you since that evening I saw you in Little Ron's, dressed in your waitress's skintight black minidress with your golden hair cascading over your shoulders. Now I know that a girl wants to be appreciated as a person and not simply as a sex object, but I would be lying in my teeth if I did not tell you that the minute I saw you, my whole body began to tingle all over and, in seconds, a huge bulge formed in my lap as my cock stood up as ramrod stiff as a guardsman on sentry duty outside Buckingham Palace.

Just as I started penning this note, I was thinking about you and how hard you must work, always being at the customers' beck and call, lugging heavy trays of food and all the time having to smile brightly, even though you've been on your feet for the last five hours.

Let me tell you about a little fantasy which has been in my mind for the last few days. I would pick you up from the restaurant and drive us to my flat, where I'd carry you into the bedroom and slide my hands over your glorious bum cheeks before unzipping your dress and pulling it down to the ground. With a sensuous smile, you reach behind and unhook your bra and I tenderly smooth the straps down over your shoulders. Then I sink to the floor on my bended knees as, with trembling hands, I slowly pull down your knickers and thrill to the sight of your lovely honey-coloured bush. I know that I have yet to see it, but I imagine that your pink, pouting pussy lips are covered by a thick triangular thatch of silky blonde hair, neatly trimmed and already moist as gingerly I stroke your long gash with my fingertips.

By now, my prick is rock hard and throbbing like crazy and so now I lead you to the bed and you lie spreadeagled on the cool, white sheets whilst I tear off the rest of my clothes. Now when I am as naked as you, I slide a pillow under your bottom to elevate your delectable pussy and I jump up between your legs and, without further ado, ease my tongue into you and lick and lap around your cunny, tantalising your clitty until you scream for my cock to thrust itself inside your dripping love hole.

I rise up and slide my big cock all the way in until our hairs are mingling together. I would allow you a few moments to get accustomed to the size of my pulsating prick, and then I set up a slow rhythm, sliding my cock in and out of your juicy lovebox which has you arching your back and screaming with delight. Then I quicken the pace until you are writhing underneath me and I can feel your cunny walls clamping and releasing my shaft until, with one almighty heave, I flood your cunt with a boiling river of spunk and you scream out your ecstasy as an electric climax courses through you whilst I cream your cunny in a glorious mutual orgasm.

Wendy, darling, I can hardly wait for tonight – the London to Glasgow express may not be the most romantic place to consummate our relationship, but I shall have impatiently counted the hours to when we will be making love and my fantasy will turn into fabulous reality.

All my love,
Antony

Wendy folded the sheets neatly back into the book which she carefully replaced on top of Antony's case. Then she silently padded into the small bathroom and showered. When she returned, a large towel draped around her shoulders and over her back, she dried herself facing the full-length mirror inside the open door of the wardrobe, and Wendy smiled knowingly when she noticed Antony begin to stir. She let the towel fall and stood naked in front of the mirror as she took off her shower cap and, bending forward slightly, she combed out her long blonde strands of silky hair. Antony was now awake and he sat up as he gazed upon Wendy's splendidly polished, lithe body, the globes of her bottom round and smooth, her breasts high and proud as she now stood upright, stock still as she saw that he was looking so longingly at her.

She turned and walked purposefully towards the bed. Antony opened his mouth to speak but she placed her finger gently against his lips as she mounted him, and let her body wriggle lasciviously against him as she placed her lips against his and wordlessly they embraced as their tongues made darting journeys of exploration inside each other's mouths.

Antony purred like a cat as Wendy moved her luscious body across him, the tips of her breasts brushing deliciously against his own nipples as she slid downwards until her mouth was level with the base of his heavy shaft, which had partially swelled but not yet sprung to more than a semi-erect state.

With an unhurried calm she lapped around his knob, grasping his shaft with one hand, sliding her fingers up and down the hot, thickening pole whilst with the other she gently massaged his balls. This skilful coaxing broke through his mental block and Antony's prick suddenly sprang upwards, quivering with desire as it curved upwards, and Wendy opened her mouth and sucked in as much of his throbbing shaft as she could between her rich, red lips which brought a low, wrenching groan of ecstasy from him. She bobbed her head backwards and forwards, uninhibitedly sucking noisily on his bursting cock until she sensed that he was edging towards a climax.

Now she took his twitching tool out of her mouth and pulled him across her as she parted her long, slim legs and with her fingers, invitingly spread open the pink lips of her juicy honeypot. Antony mounted her eagerly, savouring the moment as he gave his wet prick a final rub before guiding his cock into her lush pussy, and Wendy raised her legs high in the air as he came into her. Their loins were locked together and they made love with total abandon. He fucked the delicious girl in long, smooth strokes and his balls slapped in cadence against her backside as he moved up and down, rubbing her stalky nipples as his cock squelched in and out of her sopping cunt.

'I'm coming! Oh yes, I'm coming, darling!' Wendy yelled out happily as the dizzying circles of pleasure which emanated from between her legs widened and widened. 'Spunk into my cunny now and fill me up with your hot, sticky jism!'

Antony spent immediately, spurting his spunk inside her pulsating pussy and this sent Wendy right over the edge, launching her into a shattering orgasm, and her body bucked wildly whilst Antony worked his prick in and out of her drenched cunny until the last drops of sperm were milked from his deflating shaft.

Now Antony was rampant and, within minutes, his thick prick was standing stiffly upwards from its thicket of curly dark hair and he took her doggie fashion, gripping her hips as he thrust his tumescent tool deep into her cunny from behind, his shaft slewing through the crevice between Wendy's rounded bum cheeks in sharp, deep thrusts. Her fingers flew to her clitty, flicking the ripe bud as Antony now rolled and pinched her nipples in the same quickening rhythm as his pistoning strokes. Then their bodies began to shake and the tingling in Antony's cock became stronger until, with a loud cry, he jetted spurts of sticky jism inside her honeypot and Wendy's cunny quivered all round his shaft as she climaxed with him. The muscular contractions of her cunt increased his pleasure even more as his prick disgorged its flow of hot, creamy spunk and they fell forwards in an untidy heap of limbs when the delicious sensations finally subsided.

At this stage, the noise of their love-making had disturbed the foursome next door who had squeezed themselves into the double bed in Brian Lipman's compartment.

'Sounds as if some couple are having a good time,' murmured Beth sleepily as she smoothed her fingers gently over Ivor's chest before settling her head back in the crook of his shoulder and letting her hands fall down between Ivor's legs where she let her palms rub provocatively against the length of his shaft.

Brian Lipman now stirred himself and heaved himself up into a sitting position, waking up Penny whose tousled blonde hair had been sprawled over his chest whilst she slept with her back towards the photographer, her soft, curvy buttocks moulded against his side as she rested her head on his upper arm.

'What's going on?' he demanded with a puzzled expression. 'Did I hear someone scream or was I just dreaming?'

'No, you heard a girl yelling, but you can go back to sleep. I don't think she was calling for any assistance,' said Ivor with a grin, and from the adjoining compartment they listened to Wendy's final yelp of ecstasy as Antony pulled out his gleaming, semi-stiff penis from between her buttocks.

'I'm not so sure,' said Lipman grimly, disengaging himself from Penny's warm curves and sliding out of bed. He pulled on his dressing gown and said: 'I'm just going to make sure everything is kosher next door. Sorry folks, but I would never be able to forgive myself if some poor girl had been attacked and I hadn't bothered to see if I could help her.'

As he went out to investigate, quietly closing the door behind him, Penny opened her eyes and rolled over towards Ivor and Beth. 'Isn't he a good lad? Mind, I'm certain you're right, Ivor, there's no doubt in my mind about that noise coming from some lucky girl going off during a good fuck, but you have to hand it to Brian, he got up to see for himself,' she said approvingly.

Ivor nodded and said: 'He's quite right, really. You should never really ignore anything that could mean somebody is in trouble. Brian's been especially good that way ever since his old Auntie Ada's accident a couple of years ago. She's seventy-seven and lives on her own in a first-floor apartment in a block of flats. It seems that one Saturday morning the lift was out of order and the poor old dear slipped going downstairs and turned her ankle so badly that she couldn't move from where she'd fallen. She shouted for help but no-one came to find out what was wrong, even though Brian swears she must have been heard by people in at least three flats. Thank God the postman arrived and carried her back to her place or she would have been lying on the floor for the rest of the bloody day.'

'That's London for you,' said Penny with a yawn. 'You could drop dead in the road and people would simply step round your body. It was never like that in the little village in Hampshire where I grew up. On the other hand, people were so nosy that it could drive you crazy. For instance, I was involved in a terribly embarrassing situation when I was only fifteen, simply because one spring evening some interfering old busybody heard noises coming from the old hut on the village green.'

'Don't tell me you were having it away with the village bobby!' giggled Beth, and then let out a little squeal as Penny pinched her friend's bottom.

'Certainly not, he was a married man, and anyway we

all knew he was screwing Colonel Amhurst's wife. One of the girls in my class told me how her mum, who worked as a charlady at Amhurst Lodge, saw them in bed together one afternoon.

'Anyhow, what happened to me was that after supper I'd gone to the youth club in the Parish Hall and Jimmy Norris, one of the boys in my class, asked if he could walk me back home. He'd taken me to the pictures a couple of times and we'd necked in the back row, though we'd done nothing more than French kiss. Anyhow, we were both feeling randy – you know how it is at that age – and I didn't object when he steered me towards this deserted little hut which all the courting couples used. There was an old bench inside it and Jimmy and I sat down on it and started to kiss and cuddle.

'He cupped my left breast with his right hand and at first I pushed his hand away, but he kept putting it back and in the end I let it stay there because it felt so nice. Then the crafty little sod unbuttoned my blouse and slipped his hand inside – and I nearly hit the roof! I'd never let a lad touch my tits before and I was moaning with pleasure whilst I could feel a lovely tingling in my pussy and my knickers were getting wet.

'Jimmy could see that he had me going but when he tried to slide his hand up my skirt I slapped it away. But I hadn't noticed him unzipping his jeans and I almost jumped up in fright when he took hold of my hand and placed it around his naked, stiff prick which was standing up in his lap. Now I knew all about the birds and bees but I'd never actually felt a boy's stiff cock before, and it did give me a buzz to hold this hot, hard tube which throbbed away in my grasp.

'He showed me how to rub his cock but I still wouldn't let him get near my pussy, though Jimmy soon had my bra off and he was playing with my naked breasts whilst I was sliding my hand up and down his shaft.

'We were both pretty excited and we must have been panting quite noisily while we petted away. Then Jimmy let out a huge groan and suddenly my hand was covered with the hot, sticky cream which had spurted out of his knob. Now remember, everyone knew that kids used the hut to snog but old Mr Harcourt, who'd been exercising his dog on the green, thought it his civic duty to find out who was making all that noise in the old hut. Luckily, we heard his dog snuffle around the door and I managed to button my blouse and Jimmy had stuck his cock back in his jeans when Mr Harcourt opened the door and said—'

She was interrupted by Beth who gave a startled little scream because as if on cue, the compartment door opened and Brian Lipman came bustling in. 'Now then, here's a fine how-do-you-do!' he said, and his three companions immediately burst into laughter.

'Brian, you're brilliant! That's exactly what Mr Harcourt said,' cried Penny, giving the puzzled photographer a smacking great kiss on the lips.

He shrugged his shoulders. 'Well, I'm glad to have given you all a giggle, though I'm buggered if I know what's so funny. Listen, you'll never guess who's next door to us in bed with a gorgeous bird. It's Antony Godfrey, that playboy fellow who's always in the newspapers. I wonder why he's going to Glasgow?'

– TO BE CONTINUED –